THREE NIGHTS AT THE JUPITER

JOHN RYLAND

This is a work of fiction. Names, characters, places, and incidents are products of the author's imagination or are used fictitiously and are not to be construed as real. Any resemblance to actual events, locations, organizations, or persons, living or dead, is entirely coincidental.

World Castle Publishing, LLC
Pensacola, Florida
Copyright © 2024 John Ryland
Hardback ISBN: 9798323525140
Paperback ISBN: 9798891262034
eBook ISBN: 9798891262041
First Edition World Castle Publishing, LLC, May 6, 2024
http://www.worldcastlepublishing.com
Licensing Notes
All rights reserved. No part of this book may be used or reproduced in any manner whatsoever without written permission, except in the case of brief quotations embodied in articles and reviews.
Cover: Cover Designs by Karen
Cover-designs-by-karen.com
Editor: Karen Fuller

PROLOGUE TO A KILLING

Bathed in the light of a dying Coleman lamp, two fingers and a thumb gripped the handle of a coffee cup printed with large hibiscus flowers. It was dainty and feminine but much lighter than a traditional coffee mug. The cup rose from a matching saucer, guided by a weak, trembling hand that still bore the bruise from the I.V. that had been in it. When the cup met a pair of thin, pale lips, it tilted slightly. Alan Lewiston closed his eyes as he slurped the black coffee, paused, then took another careful sip.

"That's good, Mama," he said, his voice little more than a coarse whisper. He set the cup aside, and another unsteady hand came up to wipe his chin. Weakened by the cancer in his stomach and his advanced age, this was as long as he'd been out of bed in months. It didn't matter where he was, he was dying, but at least the living room was a change of scenery. Two months ago, the doctors had given him six to live. By his account, he'd never see the weather cool off.

Alan settled back in the worn-out recliner and smiled, rolling his head to the matching chair on his left. Though age and dim light hid most of her face, his wife's smile lifted his spirits. In their sixty-five years of marriage, they'd raised three kids, six dogs, and enough corn and peas to feed an army. It had been a good life, but it was coming to an end, either tonight or a few months from now.

"Let's turn the light out and get in the basement, Shug."

Alan shook his head slightly. He didn't have the energy to do much else. "You go," he said, a weak hand urging her onward. "I'm tired of hiding. I'm too old and sick to do it anymore. If I got down them damned steps, I'd never get back up again." He took a ragged breath and offered a sad smile. "I don't want to die in a damp, cold basement."

Bethel Lewiston shook her head. She'd lived with his stubbornness most of her life. "Hard-headed as ever," she said, unable to completely hide her smile. She lifted her own cup from the saucer in her hand and took a sip. "Why do you think it will come here this year? It ain't never come before."

One shoulder shrugged weakly. "I don't," Alan said. He drew in a hitched breath and let it out. "I hope it does. Maybe if it takes me, it'll get the same damned cancer I got. I hope it suffers a miserable death, too."

"Hun," she pleaded, putting a hand on his arm. "You don't even know if it works that way. It might not even come, much less catch cancer. Then all this will be for nothing. You'll have worn yourself out for nothing. If you won't go to the basement, at least let's go to bed."

Alan shrugged again. "I been hiding from that thing my whole life," he said, leaving the rest to his wife's imagination. He had been hiding, year in and year out, from the same unseen devil as everyone else he knew. So had his wife. They'd grown up on neighboring farms outside of Friendly, Alabama. Their lives were linked by proximity and the same misfortunes as everyone else. Her long raven hair was gone, and so was the strength in his back, yet here they were. Still living under the same specter, and it showed no signs of weakening with age.

"Well, if it comes here, I reckon it'll get the both of us then."

"Don't be a fool, hun. Go downstairs."

"A fool? If that ain't the pot calling the kettle black."

The corners of Alan's mouth pulled into something like a smile. Bethel always called him stubborn, but in her own ways, she was too. It was one of the things he loved about her. "I'd like to see it."

Bethel sipped her own coffee and nodded. No one had ever seen the creature that plagued their little town of Friendly, probably because if you saw it you didn't live to talk about it. Dead men tell no tales. "Folks say it's a vampire."

Alan nodded. "I reckon that's what it is, of some kind or other. Probably don't look like they do on TV."

Bethel sipped her coffee again and nodded. She sat the cup and saucer down to silence the rattling caused by her shaking hands. She offered the lie of a smile when her husband looked at her. She was scared, and despite his bravado, she knew he was too. Dying of old age, or even cancer, was one thing. Being ripped apart was a horse of another color.

As a child, she'd often wake in the midst of a nightmare screaming. It was always the same creature. Though she nor anyone else knew what it looked like, her mind had pasted bits and pieces gleaned from gossip together to form an image of what the creature looked like. The same figure haunted her mind now, all these years later.

The creature in her mind was gaunt, hunched over, its shoulders at an odd angle. It had long arms with razor-like claws dripping with blood. The legs were odd, mostly like a frog's back legs, but the toes had long claws as well. The face that haunted her dreams was dark and twisted, scarred. A mouthful of pointed teeth hung over the bottom lip. It had no hair, only a pale scalp pockmarked by scabs and patches of dark, wiry hair. The thing breathed through its open mouth, almost panting. Saliva escaped the corner of its curled back lips and hung from its chin. It moved quickly, unafraid like it knew there was nothing anyone could do to stop it.

Bethel closed her eyes as a shiver ran through her. She knew the creature probably didn't look the way she thought, but it didn't matter. It probably looked fierce enough to give her a heart attack.

"You okay?" Alan asked, looking at her with his brow furrowed. "You went all pale."

Bethel rubbed her forehead with a trembling hand. "I'm just tired, I reckon. It's getting late."

"Go to bed then."

She shook her head. "Sleep wouldn't help even if I could. I'm old, Shug. We both are. I don't know about you, but I'm tired of being scared, you know. I guess I agree with you on some points. I don't want to do this anymore. I can't."

Alan nodded. "That's why I'm sitting out here and not huddled in the basement." He reached over and took his wife's hand. "I guess if it comes, it'll get us both, and we'll be together on the other side."

She smiled. "That's something to look forward to."

"The Bible says that we'll have new bodies when we get to—" Alan stopped, looking up as a heavy thud struck the roof. He swallowed hard and looked at his wife. Her eyes were full of fear, and she was on the verge of crying. He smiled and took her hand. "It's okay, Mama."

"I want you to know that I've loved you with all my heart since the day we met."

Alan spared a glance to the back door, then looked at his wife. "Me too. I thought you were the most beautiful girl in the whole world."

Bethel ran a nervous hand over her thinning gray hair and smiled.

"I still do," he said, his eyes going back to the heavy wooden door that led to their back deck. "It'll be over quick, Mama. Don't worry."

Bethel screamed when the door burst open, spraying splinters across the room.

"Go to hell, you—" Alan's voice went silent as the creature crossed the room in an instant, wrapping long fingers around his throat. Bethel opened her mouth to scream again but never got the chance. Another hand shot out and silenced her.

Outside, darkness swallowed the town. Everyone was in their "safe place". All windows and doors were boarded up. The town was dark and silent while everyone waited restlessly for the sun to rise, bringing a close to the threat of death, at least for another year.

CHAPTER ONE

One year later
June 3rd. Early Morning.

Truman Malone looked at his reflection in the mirror and released a frustrated sigh. The knot in his black uniform tie was crooked again. Normally a mundane task, his fingers didn't want to work right. The tension, the dread had been building, and the day was finally here. Though he loathed to admit it, he was nervous.

Giving up, he slid the tie loose and pulled it from around the light blue uniform shirt, proclaiming his as an officer of the Friendly Police Department, Friendly, Alabama. Leaning forward on the sink, he dropped his head with a heavy sigh.

There were only a few times that made him hate being a police officer. Meeting politicians was one, belligerent citizens were another, but the worst would begin today. He hated the first few weeks of June. The very thought of it knotted his stomach.

He turned, looking into his room as a knock came at his door. Living on the third floor of a hotel had its advantages. He got clean towels every day and clean linens twice a month, and he rarely got unexpected guests.

Tossing the tie onto the bathroom counter, he went to the door. Opening it, his eyes widened at the sight of a tall red head looking back at him. Dressed in a pair of slacks and an unassuming blouse that hid her natural curves, a smile tugged at the corner of her lips as her green eyes washed over him.

She moved quickly, grabbing his shirt and pushing him back as she moved into the room. Closing the door with her foot, she spun him, pressing his back against the door. Fingernails dug into both sides of his rib cage as she threw her body against his, her lips hungrily kissing his neck.

"Well," Truman said with a smile. "Good morning to you, too."

She withdrew, putting a finger firmly to his lips. "No talking." Her hands went to the back of his neck as her body slammed into him again. One leg rose, trying to wrap around his waist as her lips met his in a frantic kiss.

"I haven't slept at all. My cravings for you have been torturous."

"You get to talk, but I don't?"

She pulled back quickly. Her brow creased deeply, her breaths coming in rapid pants. "This is no time for your silly jokes. Shut up and take me. I need to have you inside me before I die." She stretched up, finding his lips again as her hands explored his chest.

As Truman moved from the door, she climbed his body, wrapping her legs around his waist and grinding her crotch against his. "I need this so bad," she moaned as Truman carried her to the bed. He let her go, dropping her on the bed, but she held him with her legs, pulling him down with her.

Propped on his elbows, he hovered above her while her hands quickly began working the buttons on his shirt. Halfway down, her eagerness popped one loose, sending it flying.

Truman stared at the woman below him in amazement. Typically quiet and reserved, this behavior didn't fit her at all. Her eyes were afire with a ravenous lust, her body trembling with desire. Heat emanated from her body as if she might burst into flames. He'd seen her like this once before, and while he enjoyed every minute of it, the session took a toll on him. He'd ended up with several deep scratches and bite marks, as well as a pulled hamstring. He was no spring chicken, and satisfying a woman easily ten years younger than him wasn't easy. Luckily, these encounters were rare.

He lowered himself to her, pressing their bodies together, and she moaned, fingernails digging into his back. The feel of her body against his erased everything else he'd been thinking about, and there was only her. Only her enchanting green eyes, her flowing locks of red hair, her glorious, perfect body. And her savage desire.

Giving in to her, he kissed her lips roughly, pressing his growing excitement against her. His hands found her hair, clenching it in his fist as he pulled her head to the side. His mouth found her supple neck in a flurry of passionate kisses. Using her long legs to squeeze their bodies closer together as she arched her back, she closed her eyes, releasing a moan as her body shuddered with anticipation.

They both froze as four steady knocks came at his door. They were forceful, evenly spaced like a cop knocking.

Rising from her, Truman mouthed "Shit" angrily. Who could be knocking on his door this early? Only the woman below him and her father had access to the third floor.

Andria's eyes grew wide, her hands still clutching Truman. She shook her head and shrugged, beginning a silent conversation. He gave her a questioning look, asking if he should answer. Her brow creased deeply, and she shook her head adamantly. He tilted his head to the side, his eyebrows arched. Was it Jean, her father? Again, she shrugged, her eyes going to the door.

"Truman? You in there?"

Andrea closed her eyes, shaking her head. She took a deep breath and let it out silently. It was her father.

Truman nodded to her, then turned to the door. "I am, Jean, but I'm just getting out of the shower."

"Okay. Sorry to bother you, but have you seen Andrea?"

Truman looked back at her with wide eyes. Had they been caught? They both worked hard to keep their spontaneous encounters a secret. Up till now, he thought it had worked.

"Not since yesterday," Truman lied.

"Okay. No problem. I can't find her. If you see her, tell her that I cleaned up her puke from the hallway and that I don't think it's what she thought it was. I think it was maybe that sushi she ate yesterday."

"Uh, okay, Jean." Truman eyed Andrea suspiciously. "I'll let her know. If I see her, that is."

"Thank you. Come to breakfast. We have French toast. I know you love my French toast."

"Yeah. I'll do that."

"Okay, Truman. See you soon."

"You too." Truman's shoulders dropped. Both held their positions until they heard footfalls leaving the door. When the coast was clear, Andrea's legs dropped from his waist, and he flopped down on the bed beside her.

"Are you sick?" he asked.

She shook her head. "I don't know what he's talking about." She sat up, straightening her blouse.

Truman sat up, leaning forward to see her face. "You threw up?"

"Fine. A little. It's no big deal. I brushed my teeth and gargled before I came."

"While I do appreciate that, are you sick?"

"I am not sick. You heard him say it was probably the sushi."

Truman nodded, accepting the explanation. "What did you think it was?" A smile crept to his lips as he looked at her. Their last encounter was a month ago, and they rarely used protection. He worried about her getting pregnant, but he'd never brought it up.

"I am not a doctor, Truman. I have no idea." She looked away as she stood from the bed, combing her hair with her fingers.

Taking her hand before she could go far, Truman pulled her back to him. "I know you're not a doctor. But what did you *think* it was?"

"I told you that I have no idea."

"But you must have told Jean that you suspected it might be something."

"Look at you with that big goofy grin on your face. I wonder sometimes what I see in you." She smiled, taking his cheek in her hand.

"I don't know either, but whatever it is, I'm glad you do." His hands went to her hips, pulling her closer. "Now that Jean's gone," he began, kissing her stomach. "How about we pick up where we were." His hands slid to her butt, moaning as he gripped her toned backside.

"I'm sorry. I can't now. He knows I'm in here."

"No, he doesn't," Truman replied, almost pleading. "You heard him ask if I'd seen you."

Andrea smiled as she pried his hands from her butt, holding them in hers between them. "I'm sorry for any discomfort I've caused you. I don't know what's come over me lately."

"Discomfort?" Truman asked, shifting his position on her bed. "That's a nice way of saying it."

Andrea chuckled. "I truly am sorry. Perhaps I will make it up to you later."

Truman groaned. A part of him wondered what she'd do if he grabbed her, threw her on the bed, and had his way with her. He swallowed hard, considering it briefly, but decided against it. He couldn't risk it. Their relationship always felt tenuous to him, and something like that might break it altogether.

"I should go. I'm sorry."

Truman watched her go, crestfallen. "Shit," he said after the door closed. Today was already going to suck. Now, it would be even worse.

CHAPTER TWO

June 3rd. Morning.

Downtown was already a hotbed of activity despite the early hour. There was no excitement, only the usual sense of urgency and fear. People were going through a well-rehearsed routine as they prepared for the seminal event of the year. It was that time of year again in Friendly, Alabama, but no one was celebrating.

As he rolled through the streets in his police cruiser, Truman Malone took it all in with a veteran's eye. He'd seen all this too many times to count. Well, he could count them but didn't care to.

When he married and moved to this place, his hair was dark and full. Now, it was neither. He wore a smattering of gray, gracing his temples with no shame. He'd been around the block enough times to gain some wisdom.

He knew who might need an extra set of hands and who didn't, who needed some quiet reassurance to calm their nerves, and who would be mad about the whole situation. Those citizens never bothered him. The ones that pained his heart were the people who were quietly going about the chore of preparation. Those people had truly accepted what would happen and didn't complain at all. They reminded him of an old plow horse, broken and resigned to its fate.

All the apprehension, the oddness of the situation, had given way to a silent acceptance. So many people had never known anything else, having been born and raised here. For them, to not go through an early June in this manner would be strange.

He knew people who'd moved away. There were plenty of them. Did they look at their calendars and see that it's June 3rd and stop and think about those still here? Did it even give them pause, no longer being a part of the whole ordeal? He thought that it would. If you ever lived in Friendly for any length of time, you always took a part of it with you. You just didn't tell anyone about it.

Truman sighed, shaking his head. Even now, after so many years, the whole situation still felt surreal, like something out of a movie. The weeks surrounding June fourth were always full of anxiety as the push to get prepared took over the town. Some people quietly remembered the date from past years, while others hoped and prayed that this year wouldn't be memorable for them.

His eyes went to a flatbed truck parked too close to the corner of Second Avenue and Mulberry Street. A stack of battered plywood sat next to it on the manicured lawn of a two-story Craftsman that belonged to the Simmons family. He could write the driver a ticket, but he wasn't going to, and everybody knew it.

On the bed of the truck were more stacks of plywood, and plywood was a valuable commodity in Friendly, Alabama today. In many ways, it was the most valuable commodity in town.

As he rolled slowly past, he found two young men in blue tee shirts. Scott's Construction was written across their chests in yellow block lettering. Both young men, probably fresh out of high school, already had sweat rings around their necks. Neither looked at him as he rolled slowly past.

One of them checked the clipboard in his hand and then passed it to Buford Simmons. The man whose wallet was normally as tight as the bark on a tree, signed the clipboard and handed one of them a check with a smile on his face. The young man slipped the check under the clip, tossed the whole thing into the cab of the truck, and yelled to his compadre, already in the process of strapping down the remaining plywood.

From the looks of the amount of wood still on the truck, they had several more stops to make. They'd probably finish it and get a new load, working right up to curfew. Allowing enough time to get home before dark, of course. No one wanted to be out after dark.

Scott Billows, of Scott's Construction, made a good but fair living off the same few hundred sheets of plywood. Every year, starting on June first, his men would begin deliveries. Stacks of plywood would start showing up at houses around town. For Truman, sighting the first stack was like seeing the first robin of spring or the first bright head of a daffodil, only far less welcomed.

The stacks varied in size, depending on how many doors and windows the house had. Scott's customers got enough to secure every one of them. Every last entry would be boarded shut, and the people would disappear for nearly three days.

Following the mantra of "what goes up must come down," the same men would pick up the plywood in four days and haul it back to Scott's shop. Of course, all of this was done for a fee, but people paid it willingly. It beat storing a dozen or so sheets of heavy, hard-to-handle plywood yourself. Most people simply didn't have the space, the muscle, or the willingness to do it.

Scott also had a crew that would install it on every opening in a client's house, then remove it when the time came, but that was a different crew. They were the really busy ones, especially today. It was a race against the clock.

All eight hundred sixty-seven people who lived in

Friendly, Alabama, were preparing for the annual sequester. It was the biggest event of the year, though it lacked the excitement of the Fourth of July festival or the pageantry of the Christmas parade. The sequester was met mostly with a watchful eye, not discussed as much or even welcomed. Groups of old women didn't sit around planning it. Nobody gave speeches at Civitan Park. There were no potluck dinners or ceremonies. Plywood was the only decoration.

The sequester just came and went as unceremoniously as the winter rains or the summer heat. Through the years, it had become a fact of life, akin to hurricanes for people living on the Gulf Coast. Nobody liked it, but it happened anyway. Every year without fail for as long as anyone could remember. Thus was life in Friendly.

The brakes on Truman's car squeaked as he rolled to a stop at a traffic light. His eyes followed an elderly woman and a young man crossing the street in front of him. Mrs. Wooden was a widow, and her son, Mark, had moved back home from Birmingham after his father's death to help her out with things.

Mark's father, a pig-headed, stubborn old man, was raised in the ways of his own pig-headed, stubborn father, which was the reason Mark moved away in the first place. Mark being gay and all. But, of course, that was the worst-kept secret in town.

Truman smiled, offering a wave as they passed in front of him. Mark smiled and waved back. His mother simply cast a harsh stare in his direction, her lips pursed beneath her hawk-like nose. Never exactly what you'd call "sociable," Mrs. Wooden's temperament seemed to get worse with each passing year.

Truman sighed, shaking his head as he watched them make the far sidewalk. He didn't envy the kid being sequestered with Ester Wooden. All things considered, given the choice, he might just take his chances on the porch.

CHAPTER THREE

Preston turned his attention back to the town before him. The brick-paved road ahead of him was the official start of "Downtown." It held the original buildings, most of which were still in use. Some had even retained the upstairs balcony where it was rumored that ladies of ill repute would call to passersby, seducing them to come upstairs.

Of course, none of that went on in Friendly now. Times had changed, mostly for the better. On the corner facing him was a squatty brick structure made of mud bricks that had been painted gray. Once a saloon, it was now a furniture store. The bank of windows showed a mix of antiques and modern accommodations.

Across the street was a barber shop. Oddly enough, it had always been one. The red, white, and blue striped barber pole didn't turn anymore but still announced its presence well enough.

There was a Five & Dime store that mostly sold an odd assortment of junk and some funeral flowers. The only reason Truman ever ventured inside was either to be sociable or to get an ice-cold RC cola.

There was a jewelry store, a place that printed business cards and the like, and a few other cottage shops that catered mostly to women.

In the center of town, looming over the other buildings, was the Jupiter Hotel. His eyes found it, and he smiled, wishing his shift was over.

A polite beep from behind him pulled him back to the task at hand. He glanced in the mirror, offering an apologetic wave to the pickup truck behind him.

He rolled forward but was forced to slam on the brakes, narrowly avoiding a pickup rattling through the intersection. Crossing in front of him, the truck drew a horn blast from an SUV coming from the opposite direction. The woman driving it threw her hands up at him, jerking a thumb in the direction the truck had gone. Truman grunted, muttering under his breath, and flipped on his lights. Turning left, he went after the truck.

When the truck pulled into the Super Saver parking lot, he pulled in behind it. He didn't bother calling it in or grabbing his ticket book. Truman knew the driver, and although the kid deserved it, he wasn't going to write him a ticket anyway.

Getting out of his car, he surveyed the occupants through the dirty back glass of the truck. There was some movement inside the cab, but not enough to cause alarm. They were probably just hiding a joint or two. The two occupants were likely Dusty Frasier and Mason Biggs. Pot was their drug of choice, but they never had enough money to buy much at one time.

The two of them were thick as thieves and always seemed to be up to something that didn't sit right with most of the people in the quiet, conservative community that Friendly had become. Most of it he could shrug off as youthful exuberance, but sometimes they did go too far. Like now.

"Dusty," Truman said as he approached the elbow hanging out of the driver's side window.

"That light was yellow, man," he complained without looking at Truman.

"We both know it wasn't, Dusty. C'mon."

"Whatever, bruh."

Truman looked at the driver. In his late twenties, a scruffy beard clung to his chin. Oily, sandy brown hair hung well past his shoulders. A gold chain lay on his bare, freshly sunburned chest. Dusty held a general disdain for the police, and most of the time, the feeling was mutual.

In a town as small as Friendly, there were few secrets. Truman knew both young men in the truck had gone through several dead-end jobs since high school, never keeping any of them long. They liked smoking pot and hanging out at the swimming hole much more than they liked gainful employment.

Truman's eyes darted to the passenger, likewise shirtless and wearing a pair of dirty jeans and cowboy boots. He, too, had been in the sun too long, enjoying the last days before the sequester began.

"Mason," he said. "How're the folks?" The Biggs were a respectable family who carried a fair amount of shame for the way their youngest son turned out. Mason's older brother had ridden his baseball prowess to a junior college upstate and had gotten a degree. The last time he talked to Wilson Biggs, their father, the man had proudly told him about his son's latest promotion. Wilson didn't mention Mason at all, and neither did Truman.

"They're good," Mason replied, dropping his eyes to his hands. "Thanks for asking."

"Good. Good." Mason tapped on the door of the truck with his knuckle. "Look, Dusty, I'm just going to give you a verbal warning, okay? Be careful, man. The last thing you want is to cause a wreck and end up owing a bunch of money. Or worse, catching a charge for vehicular manslaughter and end up down in Atmore for the next twenty years."

"The light was yellow, bruh."

Truman stared at the kid, fighting the urge to smack him in the face. That's what he needed. Maybe then he'd finally grow up some. "Whatever. Look, just be careful, okay? Lots of people out, lots going on, as I'm sure you know. Just take it easy. Be careful."

"Well, maybe if the po-lice worried about the things that matter instead of rousting innocent drivers, there wouldn't be so much going on."

Truman forced a smile, absorbing the comment with as much decorum as he could muster. "All the same, Dusty. Just be more careful."

"All the same, nothing. My uncle was killed last year, and y'all ain't done shit about it."

Truman sighed, hooking his thumbs in his utility belt. Dusty's uncle had been killed during the last sequester, but nothing Truman had heard led him to believe that they were close. Like his brother, Alvin Biggs was ashamed of his nephew and had little to do with him.

"I am sorry for your loss, Dusty. I truly am, but there's nothing we can do about that, and you know it."

"You could go out and hunt for that damned thing."

"That is one option. But there's only five of us, including the chief, and he's pushing seventy. We don't even know where to begin looking. Besides, we'd need a hell of a lot more manpower. Maybe we could get a few volunteers. Would you care to put your name on the list?"

The young man scoffed. "I ain't getting myself killed. I ain't no po-lice man."

A wry smile slid across Truman's face. "Okay then. That's what I thought. Have a nice day now. Mason, give my regards to the folks." Truman turned and started toward his cruiser.

"And, hey, fix your damned button, fatass!"

Truman looked down at his shirt, remembering the button Andrea had torn away in her eagerness to undress him. He sighed and walked on to his car, ignoring the laughter coming from the truck as it drove away.

He got into the car and slammed the door hard. "This day just keeps getting better," he sighed. He'd felt angry and frustrated all morning and wanted to blame it on the way it started, but he knew that wasn't it.

The problem wasn't Andrea or even those punks. The real problem was that there was nothing to do about what would happen soon, and any sane person knew it. He took the angry words in stride as best he could. People were understandably scared and frustrated. So was he. He didn't like the sequester any more than anyone else. He just happened to be one of the ones wearing a badge. That meant he also had to wear the blame, like it or not.

The radio in his car squawked to life as he watched the truck speed away. He lifted the mouthpiece from its cradle with a reluctant sigh. "Malone. Go ahead."

"Hey, Truman, you busy?"

"Yessir," Truman answered, recognizing his boss' gruff voice. "I'm very busy. Extremely busy. Much too busy to possibly do anything else," Truman said with a flat smile.

"Good. That's good. But I don't care. You have to come to this meeting with me. We've got an appointment with a huge asshole."

"I'm no proctologist, sir." Truman rolled his eyes, wanting anything but a meeting today.

"Me neither, but all the same, he wants a meeting."

"I assume you're talking about our illustrious mayor."

"The one and only. Who the hell else would want a chat right now when we're so damned busy? You're the deputy chief, so you better get used to the fun side of police work. It's not all glitz and glamour, you know. Today you get to listen to a puffed-up jackass pretend like he has some real authority."

"Well, I was going to poke a hornet's nest with a stick…"

"As fun as that sounds, it'll have to wait."

"Well, if you insist."

"I do. Come by the station and pick me up."

"My pleasure," Truman lied. He replaced the radio with a groan. Meetings were always so boring and fruitless, especially ones with the mayor. He'd been elevated to deputy chief five years ago out of sheer attrition, but the small bump in pay wasn't enough to cover the additional headaches. The only good thing about the position was that he only had to pull an occasional night shift.

Typically, the job was quiet and easy. An occasional parking ticket, and sometimes a speeding citation. Every now and then, a man would have a little too much to drink and slap his wife around, and they'd have to haul him to jail. Even then, the guy always went peacefully. Usually, his wife would be waiting on them at nine a.m. to bail him out the next morning.

There wasn't much to do. Most people were amicable and followed the rules. Friendly, Alabama was, more or less, friendly. Most of the year, anyway.

Truman rubbed his eyes with his fingertips, then moved to his temples. If anything good would come of the sequester, it would be the time off. His mind was tired, his body was tired, and all of a sudden, he was feeling his age.

Sitting back with a sigh, Truman looked around the parking lot. People were coming and going with little sense of urgency. Old hands at this, people knew exactly how much time they needed to finish up and get home. They were stocking up on food and snacks for the sequester. Being shut up with your family for nearly three days was bad enough. Doing it without your favorite chips or a big ole bag of M&Ms would be torture.

Watching the people come and go with their grocery bags, he wondered how many of them were buying milk and loaf bread, a staple people always rushed out to get when the odd forecast of snow came their way. He never understood the reasoning behind it, but it happened every time.

His eyes landed on two women, a blond on her way in and a brunette on her way out. When they stopped to talk in the parking spot, the blonde said something, and they both laughed. Both women looked to be in their late twenties, probably had a husband and a couple kids. They stood in the sunshine and talked as if nothing were happening. As if they didn't have a care in the world.

Truman groaned out a sigh and started his car, wondering why this year's sequester was getting under his skin so bad. After all, this wasn't his first rodeo. Something just felt different about this year. He couldn't explain it, but he couldn't deny it either.

CHAPTER FOUR

June 3rd. Noon.

Located on the second floor of a gothic revival home donated to the city by Thurmond Newsome, a descendent of one of the town's founders, the mayor's office was much nicer than the Chief's.

The town had spent a bundle refurbishing the home to use as city hall, and from the looks of things, much of that money went to the mayor's office. Twelve-foot plaster walls gave way to a wide curved crown molding, at the center of which was a decorative strip in an egg and dart pattern.

A fan of old buildings, Truman was glad to see the place return to its former glory. However, not many people in town shared his opinion. Most people in Friendly were more frugal minded than the mayor and resented him for spending the money on what they saw as "fancy accommodations."

Truman nodded as his boss grumbled about being kept waiting, but his attention was drawn to the framed map on the wall behind the mayor's desk. At four feet by four feet, the map of Hillburn County was bigger and nicer than the one that hung in the police station lobby. It had been hand drawn with a charcoal pencil and included highlighted landmarks of the surrounding area.

His eyes found the black dot that was Friendly. Situated in the southeasternmost tip of Hillburn County, Friendly was a long way from anywhere. A fact that was driven home by the other black dots on the map. None of them were close. The nearest actual town was Akedo, which was three inches north on the map but a long half-hour drive on a winding two-lane road in real life. Not that there was much more in Akedo than there was in Friendly.

His eyes found the dark line of the Black Warrior River and followed it as it snaked its way southward in the eastern third of the county through what was mostly wilderness. The river made a big bend just north of Akedo, then wriggled south, making a nearly ninety-degree turn a few miles north of Friendly. Truman's mind went to the towboats that pushed barges of coal up and down the river, thinking that they must hate making that sharp turn.

"My apologies, gentlemen. As I'm sure you know, it's a busy time around here."

Snatched from his thoughts by the mayor's entrance, Truman forced a smile as a heavy-set man with dark hair strode into the room. He rounded the desk, unbuttoned his suit coat, and sat down in the black leather chair opposite them. Out of the corner of his eye, Truman saw that his boss didn't bother with the nicety of a smile.

Abraham Latham leaned forward, interlacing his fingers atop his expansive desk, and sighed as he looked back and forth between them. "I'm just going to get right to it, gentlemen. The general consensus is that we have to do something about this menace, this scourge that has plagued our town for far too long now."

The Police chief, a stocky but not particularly tall man, sighed loudly, voicing his displeasure without saying a word. He pushed a hand through his silvery gray hair and shook his head as he reclined in the padded chair next to Truman. The look he spared Truman told him to prepare for the fireworks.

"By general consensus, Mayor, do you by chance mean the few rich men who want to see the town grown and pad their pockets at the same time?"

"Dammit, Anthony, you know that's not true. It's just plain horseshit. That's what it is. Something must be done."

Anthony Swails shrugged one shoulder. "Maybe it is crap, maybe it's not, but I'm betting not."

"Damned you. You think everything is about money and power. Power and money. That's all you ever say. Shit. We can't keep burying our heads in the sand every year. I don't even know why you bother to come to these meetings."

"Maybe I just want to see what an expensive suit looks like up close." A defiant smile slipped across Anthony's weather-beaten face. He'd been elected to eight straight four-year terms as Chief of Police and had enough clout of his own to not have to worry about political pressure from the mayor.

"You're just an asshole. Did you know that?"

"If I had a dollar every time someone told me that, I'd be a rich man, I reckon," Anthony said, locking eyes with the mayor.

"Look," Truman said, hoping to diffuse the growing tension. There was no love lost between the two small-town leviathans, and neither tried very hard to hide it. Both had been in office for a long time by appealing to two very different electorates.

The average, working-class people were loyal to Anthony. The few that had money used it to reelect the mayor. It was a clash of clans as old as the town itself.

"Everyone wants this thing to stop," Truman began. "I'm sure no one wants it to continue. I sure as hell don't. The problem is that we're all virtually helpless, and everybody knows it."

The Chief acquiesced with a nod. The mayor shook his

head.

"We simply must do *something*. That's the long and short of it. It's only a matter of time before the town begins to wither and die. Some people think we're past that point already. Is that what y'all want?"

"Nobody wants that," Truman replied flatly.

"I suppose you have a plan," Anthony said dryly, looking at Abraham Latham with his eyes narrowed.

"Well, nothing concrete," he answered weakly. "But that's not my department. I don't have access to the armory."

"Armory?" Anthony asked with a chuckle. "You mean the five shotguns, hundred or so shells, and the five side arms that we carry? That armory?"

"You know what I mean, Anthony. Why are you so obstinate?"

"Abe, listen close. You can use all the big words you want, and it won't change a thing. We've been down this road before. Most of the men in this town outgun the five of us easily. Our budget is so lean that we can't even afford to do target practice, let alone replace outdated ammunition."

"Times are lean. Tax revenues have fallen for three straight years." The mayor nodded as he looked between them. "Which only goes to reinforce my point. Something must be done."

Anthony shook his head. "We aren't trained for things like that. Hell, no one is. Who could be?"

"Still," The mayor persisted. "We have to do… something." He waved his hand at Anthony.

"I'd be willing to listen to any suggestions," Truman said.

"I don't know." Abraham leaned back in his chair and wiped his face with both hands. "The city council met this morning and has come up with some suggestions. Maybe a trap of some kind. You know, lure the thing in."

Anthony scratched his head and smoothed his hair, taking

a moment to compose himself. "This thing can rip a metal door off its hinges, and you want us to prop up a box with a stick, tie a string to it, and pull it when it goes inside?" He turned to Truman. "Hell, maybe we can bait it with a sign that says free food."

"Don't be insipid, Anthony. Hell, that's not what I meant, and you damned well know it."

"It makes about as much sense as it does on cartoons. Probably work out about the same, too, if you ask me." The chief grunted. "A trap. We're not dealing with a rabbit or a freaking sparrow here."

"You're just being difficult. You know that's not what I meant."

"I also know it's stupid as hell." The chief sat up in his chair. "How big does the trap need to be, Abe? Tell me that. Did the city council have any suggestions on the subject? What will it be made of? Any idea? Steel? Wood? Titanium? And who's going to build it? And then, and then, if some fucking miracle happens and we do catch it, what in the hell do we do then?" He shook his head. "Who is going to stand out there and operate it? I'll tell you one thing, it sure as hell won't be me or one of my officers."

"You've sworn an oath to serve and protect this town!"

"And I can't do that if I get my guts ripped out, you damned fool!"

"Gentlemen," Truman interjected. "I'll agree that the plan to trap this thing is fraught with dangers, but it might have some merit to it."

"Really?" Anthony asked, looking at his deputy chief.

"I don't know. Hell, I'm really just trying to make sure you two don't come to blows, to be honest." He turned to the mayor. "Abe, I know people want us to do something. I get it from folks all the time. It's always this time of year. People get antsy, pissed off, and voice their frustration. Believe me, I feel the same way they do."

"See," Abe said, pointing a finger at Truman as he glared at the chief.

"But," Truman continued, "What, realistically, can we do? What feasible plan is there? We are a small-town police force with very limited resources." He looked between the two men, both of whose cheeks were red with frustration and anger. "We all know what happened the last time a group of folks tried to do something."

"Yes. Six men died. Three of them were shot by their own buddies in the chaos when they panicked. One of them nearly had his head blown plumb off."

The mayor sighed, rubbing his chin. "That was years ago."

"Do you think this thing has gotten kinder, gentler since then? Hell, maybe we can just ask it to stop, and it will. Say please and thank you. Hell, let's tell it that we don't feel validated and that it makes us uncomfortable."

"Don't be preposterous, Anthony. Shit."

"Me? You're asking me to go out and fight something that we can't even identify. We don't even know what the hell it is!" He pointed at the mayor. "What we do know is that it's fast, powerful, and has claws, and apparently loves to drain its victims of every fucking drop of their blood. It might be two feet tall, might be twenty for all we know. It might weigh ten pounds or five hundred."

"That's true," Truman added. "I've been through a lot of these—"

"And so have I," the mayor snapped.

"Yeah," Anthony said, "But we don't do it from behind a fucking fancy desk. We're the ones who collect the bodies and take them to the morgue. We see the blood, the body parts. The violence. We see what this thing does to a human body."

Truman nodded. "It's every bit as bad as people say.

Worse, really."

"Don't you see? That's even more reason to do something. We can't just sit by and let this continue."

"You're the freaking mayor, Abe. Why don't *you* do something? Call the state police, the governor? Hell, anyone. The unvarnished truth of it is that we cannot handle this thing. Going after it will only get more people killed. Holing up and waiting it out has worked."

"Not for the two or three people it takes out every year."

"Would you rather it be ten? Twenty?"

"I'd rather it be none!" The mayor slammed his fist on his desk. "Shit, Anthony, the town is dying. Look around. People are moving away, especially the younger folks. Who would want to raise a family under this specter?"

"Again, what would you have us do?"

"It's not that we're unwilling," Truman said. "It's just that everything we've come up with has failed miserably. The high-pitched siren didn't keep it away. The searchlights didn't work. The smoke didn't work. Hell, the hundred or so trail cameras we put up around town last year didn't even catch a glimpse of this thing. It's smart and powerful. The chief is right. Even after all this time, we still don't have a clue what we're up against."

Abraham Latham sighed, shaking his head. "We all know damned well what it is. Y'all just don't want to admit it."

"Don't even start that same old shit with me, Abe."

"It's a vampire, and you know it, Anthony. Everybody knows it."

"You don't know shit, but I'll tell you what I do know. I know you watch too many damned movies. Vampires do not exist. They are not real. It's also not a big foot. It's not a Rougarou. It's not a Wendigo. It's none of those things because they don't exist." Anthony raised his voice on the last three words for emphasis.

"Then why does it drink the blood?" Abe asked, one eyebrow raised as if he'd won the point. "Tell me that."

"Who says it drinks it? Maybe it just drains them and takes it off in a fucking Home Depot bucket."

"Good lord, man." Abe straightened his tie as he adjusted his position in his chair. "You're just being ridiculous."

"And you're acting like a scared little schoolgirl."

"All the blood wouldn't even fit in a bucket, dumbass," Abe shot back.

"Actually, the average adult body only contains about one and a half gallons of blood," Truman put in. When both men looked at him questioningly, he shrugged. "What? I research stuff. It's called the internet, folks. I'm old, but not that old."

"Whatever," Anthony said, turning back to the mayor. "What you're asking me to do is to try to capture or kill something that might not be able to be killed and to do it blind, with no intel. And to do it using a few old pump shotguns, the newest of which is ten years old. That sounds like a suicide mission to me."

"It's your job!"

Anthony pursed his lips tightly and shook his head. "You know what, Abe? Fine. I'll do it. If this is really what you want, I'll do it. If you want our blood on your hands, we'll do it."

"You will?" Abe asked, relief washing over his face. "It's about time you come around."

"I will," Anthony said, holding onto the mayor's gaze. "But only if you come with us."

The smile drained from Abe's face. "That's not my job."

"It's not mine either."

The mayor rubbed his face with both hands, sighing through them. "Look, Anthony, I know you don't give a shit about politics and how things look." He fell back in his chair. "People are just done with all this. They are starting to talk."

"People always talk, Abe."

"But now they're talking about our lack of action. Rumors are making their way around town. For the love of God, man. People are pointing fingers at you and me."

"For what?"

"People are starting to wonder if it's actually one of us. Or both."

"That's ridiculous. You're full of crap, Abe."

The mayor shook his head. "I wish I was." He threw his hands into the air and let them drop. "Think about it for a minute. This shit keeps happening. We're in a position to stop it, but it doesn't stop. People are wondering why we let it go on."

"Let it go on?" Anthony asked. "There's nothing we can do to stop it."

"They don't think so, and they'll let us know with their votes come next term."

"If somebody else wants this job, they can have it now."

"Anthony, I think you're doing a good job, but…"

"There's nothing that really can be done," Truman said. "And as far as rumors go, the chief has been up at the school with a couple hundred folks every year for as long as I can remember. That's a pretty good alibi."

Anthony chuckled. "Maybe *you* should account for *your* whereabouts, Abe. Maybe it's you." He patted his belly with both hands. "You're looking awful plump."

"I always go to the basement downstairs. There's plenty of people who'd attest to that. Jackass."

"Well then. There you have it."

"People don't care about that. They just want to stop burying their friends and family every damned year."

"Then I suggest you make some calls, Abe."

"You're the police chief. Do your job."

"Well." The chief stood and motioned for Truman to join him. "When I see the motherfucker run a stop sign, I'll be sure to write it a ticket." He turned and stormed out the door with Truman close behind.

CHAPTER FIVE

June 3rd Midday.

"You were a little rough on him, don't you think?" Truman asked as he followed his boss down the staircase toward the main floor.

"He's a dipshit and a coward on the best days, Truman. When we were younger, he was a mama's boy, and he probably still is. Never take any of his shit seriously."

"I guess, as mayor, it'd be a feather in his cap if this thing was stopped on his watch."

Anthony shook his head. "He just wants to go back to his donors and say that he fought hard, but the mean old chief adamantly refused to do anything."

"Well, we did," Truman said with a laugh.

"Yep. Just like every other time he tried to pull this crap. He and the city council sit up there in their suits and ties, talking about vampires. Hell, it might as well be zombies or some other Hollywood crap. That man wouldn't know his ass from a hole in the ground, must less what a vampire looks like."

"Well, it has to be something, doesn't it?"

"Oh, it's something. Something I don't want to face with these pea shooters," he said, swiping a hand at the forty-five-caliber pistol on his hip. "Notice that he didn't volunteer himself or any of his rich buddies to go with us?"

"I did notice," Truman said with a grin. As they reached the landing, his boss stopped and turned back to him.

"Look, I know folks are antsy. Hell, I am, too. Who ain't? But my hands are tied. It's the choice of two losses. It's shit or more shit, Truman. That's what it is. There's no winning. You know that."

"I know. And I agree." Truman waited as a middle-aged woman made her way down the hallway and out the door next to them, giving her a smile and a nod as she passed them. "I mean, people have been giving me crap for years, especially around this time of year. I even got it from that kid, Dusty Frazier, not an hour ago. Everybody's on edge."

"I know." Anthony scratched the back of his head. "It sucks being on the receiving end, but I hear them out. I let them get it off their chest. They've got a right to be mad, or scared, or frustrated. Or all of the above. Hell, I'm all those things, too."

Truman nodded. "It's an impossible situation if you ask me."

"Yep, but they don't see what we see. Do they? They go to the funerals and see a closed casket. They don't see Mrs. Jones' chest ripped open or Mr. Abernathy's face that's ghostly white because he has no blood left in him. Hell, he was my history teacher when I was in school, Truman. I know these people and have for years. Don't you think it bothers me to see them like that?"

"I'm sure it does," Truman said. "I know it does."

"And assholes like these dipshits," he jerked a thumb back up the stairs, "they don't really give a shit."

"I'm sure they're affected like everyone else."

"Like every other politician, they're insulated from the shit we have to deal with. It's easy to come up with a plan if you're not the one implementing it. His ass will never be in danger."

"True," Truman agreed with a shrug.

"But." The chief turned and pushed through the front door and stepped onto the small porch outside. "The thing is, I can't afford to react out of fear or emotion. Or pressure from political donors. I have to decide whether or not to send men out to what I know in my heart is going to be a slaughter. Men who have families. Men who don't want to go. Deep down, I think everyone in town knows that too."

"I hope so."

"I know so because when folks are bitching at me, or you, and they have all these great ideas about how to kill it, do they ever volunteer to come with us?"

"Not a one," Truman said with a dry smile. "As a matter of fact, I just asked that kid Dusty the same thing, and he changed his tune awful quick."

"Exactly." The chief stabbed a finger at him as he started down the steps toward the police cruiser parked on the street. "People just want to vent, to feel like they're doing something. Hell, I get it. Do you think that my wife doesn't give me an ear full every time one of the old bats in her sewing circle, or somebody they know gets it? She does. She goes on and on about it until I get abate of hearing it and tell her to shut the hell up."

He stopped and turned back to Truman. "I'm on blood pressure medicine. I take a pill for my nerves every day. Hell, I'll even admit to you that I drink too much sometimes. I sleep like shit from late May all the way through June. I hate this shit, probably more than most because, ultimately, every one of those deaths falls on my shoulders."

"That's not true, Chief. You can't think about it like that. There's nothing you can do."

The chief shrugged and continued down the steps.

"It doesn't make sense," Truman said, following him. "Us guys talk amongst ourselves. They don't want to go out and fight this thing. Like you said, they both have kids. Allen has a toddler."

"What about you?"

Truman shook his head. "No wife or kids, remember? But all the same, I'd like for my internal organs to stay internal."

"That's reassuring."

"I mean, we'd probably do it if you told us to."

"Probably?"

"Well, we all say we would go if you went, but when push comes to shove, and wives start talking in ears…" Truman tossed his hands into the air. "I'm not too proud to admit that the thought of seeing it scares the hell out of me."

"Well, tell the boys not to worry. I'm not going to order them to get themselves killed."

"That's good to know." Truman wiped the sweat from his brow and cast an accusing look at the sun. June had just started, and the heat was already pushing ninety degrees. "Anyway, I just don't get it. I mean, why June fourth? Why not Halloween or the summer or winter solstice? What's so special about that date?"

"Damned if I know." The chief reached the sidewalk and took a handkerchief from his back pocket. He wiped his face and then jammed it back where he'd gotten it from. He looked at Truman and shrugged. "Maybe it's some biological thing."

"I doubt it." Truman shook his head as he rounded the car. He slid in behind the wheel and started the car, turning the air conditioner on high.

"Biological responses like migration, feeding patterns, stuff like that are all cyclical but never fall on the same date. They usually follow temperature changes or lunar cycles, and the full moon changes throughout the year."

"You have been spending some time on the internet."

"I don't have a television in my room, and there's only so many times you can read the newspaper."

"I figured you'd find ways to keep busy with the old man's daughter down there at the hotel. I've been by there a time or two. I've seen her." The chief's eyebrows rose as he looked at Truman, smiling. "She's quite the looker."

Truman shook his head, smiling. "She's a busy woman, I guess."

"She's a right pretty thing, I'll say that much."

"That she is," Truman agreed with a smile.

"How come you ain't married her yet?"

"I'll just say she's hard to pin down and leave it at that."

"The prettiest ones always are."

Truman nodded, intentionally changing the subject. "I don't know that all my research helped at all."

"Well," the chief said with a sigh. "I've done the same thing time and time again. I've talked to the old folks. I've talked to the state folks about any cults that might be around." He shook his head. "Nothing. Hell, once I even called this demonologist fella. He was about as helpful as tits on a bull. That's just between you and me, by the way."

Anthony rubbed his eyes and then wiped his mouth with the palm of his hand. "You find anything special on the internet?"

"Nothing that stands out." Truman sighed, recalling some of the events he'd uncovered. "I mean, there's tons of stuff about rituals and stuff like that, but, like I said, they're mostly in conjunction with a luminary event. Nothing whatsoever about June fourth. I mean, it's two days before D-day. Mickey Mantle hit a five hundred fifty-foot homer off some guy." Truman shrugged. "And Kennedy got shot."

"John?"

Truman shook his head. "Bobby."

"Well, there you have it."

"I know, but it just doesn't make sense. If it were an animal of some kind and woke from hibernation and started to feed, it would start earlier than this. Maybe sometime in March, and it would keep happening all summer."

"Look, I've run myself half nuts trying to figure this shit out. I've spent a thousand sleepless nights thinking about what it could be. You will, too. The truth of it is that it happens every June fourth like clockwork, and we can't do shit to stop it. Not one damned thing. The mayor might not like hearing it, but that's the truth."

"The crazy thing is that other than that one day, this town is a pretty nice place to live. Quiet. Good people."

The chief looked at Truman. "Yep. Maybe that's the only reason why there's still a town left."

"You ever run across any of the old timers who knew anything? I mean, like when it all started?"

The chief shook his head, his eyes staring out the windshield at the historical marker standing on the lawn in front of the home that now served as City Hall.

"You ever look up the town's history?"

"Some. Not much to see."

The chief nodded toward the marker. "This old fart, Thurston, whatever his name was. His grandfather was one of the original group of folks that founded this town. They say it was a hell of a rough place back then. Full of outlaws and swindlers taking advantage of people traveling west as the country opened up."

"I know that part. Kinda hard to believe now." Truman's eyes washed over the manicured lawn in front of city hall to the azalea bushes that stood on both sides of the steps. The house looked like so many others in town.

"Did you know this place used to be called Red Hill?"

"Red Hill? Why that?"

"Who the hell knows? All the red clay around these parts, maybe. Back then, there was all kinds of boozing, gambling, whoring, and all kinds of bad stuff going on. After a few years, the place got a reputation, I guess. The only folks who came here were other outlaws and gunslingers looking for an easy mark themselves."

"You don't say."

The chief laughed. "I guess if you rob and shoot enough people, word gets out. Anyway, folks started avoiding Red Hill altogether. Them assholes got together one day and set out to figure a way to get folks to keep passing through. They only had two ferries in the county back then. One was up in Souls Harbor, the other was here. If you wanted to cross the river, that was it for a hundred miles in either direction."

"What'd they do?"

"They changed the name of the town."

Truman laughed. "And they settled on Friendly?"

"Can you think of a better way to pretend like they weren't going to rob you, maybe cut your throat?"

"Damn. That's savage right there."

"Yeah." Anthony chuckled as he nodded. "Eventually, the law came, and things started to settle down. Statehood and all that. Now it's the thriving metropolis we all know and love, but the name stuck."

"You think that's why this thing came here?" Truman asked.

"Came here, born here. Who the hell knows? But if I was looking for a place to do shit like that, a town like the one this one used to be would be a perfect place to hide in plain sight."

"That could go on for years before anyone really put it together. It could drop the bodies in the woods or the river, and no one would ever know."

Anthony nodded in agreement. "And it's been happening ever since."

"I wonder how many people have been killed."

"Too many to count would be my guess." Anthony Swails shook his head. "So, you see why I'm not keen on adding any more names to that list?"

"I'm not arguing that."

"Look, I wish it wasn't like this. Believe you me, I wish it wasn't. But it is. All we can do is keep as many people as safe as we can and spare their loved ones from seeing them like that. Whether or not the mayor likes it, that's it. End of story."

"What the hell is wrong with you?"

Truman jumped, nearly spilling the glass of sweet tea he'd been idly stirring with a straw. His mind was still on his conversation with the chief, and he didn't see the woman approach his booth. He looked up as Rhonda Trammel, the wife of an old friend, slid into the seat across the table from him.

"Hello to you, too."

"Hello, Truman." Rhonda gave him a quick smile. "Now, what's wrong with you?"

Truman looked at her and shrugged. "Well, right now, I've got a headache from having a round with the freaking mayor. But generally speaking, my cholesterol is a little high, and my blood pressure tends to run up there from time to time. I sometimes get an ache in my lower back, but that's probably from these crappy uniform shoes. They have very little arch support, you know."

"Ha, ha," she said, screwing up her face at him. "That's not what I'm talking about, and you know it."

"I'm not sure I do. It's been a long day already," Truman replied. He knew perfectly well what she was talking about but hoped to dodge the question. Rhonda was friends with Tiffany Jasper and had gone out of her way to make sure they met at the St. Patrick's Day party she'd thrown back in March.

"Tiffany told me you ended things with her."

Truman shrugged, sipping his tea instead of responding.

Rhonda threw her hands out, palms up. "What's wrong with her? She's pretty. She's smart. She's got a good job down at the bank."

"Nothing's wrong with her." Truman glanced around the diner to see who might be eavesdropping. Rhonda's voice was a natural alto and carried well.

"So, why'd you break things off? She said she thought there was something there. Y'all went on four dates." She held up her hand, her thumb tucked next to her palm. "Four good dates, from what I hear."

"I don't know. It was okay. She's fine. I just…" Truman trailed off, shaking his head.

"Well, she was pretty broken up about it. She said she likes you."

"I liked her too, well enough, I guess." Truman resumed stirring his drink.

"So, why'd you end things?"

"I don't know. There was just no spark."

"No spark? That's not what I heard. She said she bought a new dress for every date. Nice dresses. Sexy little sun dresses."

"She did always look nice."

"So?" Rhonda asked.

Truman sighed. "I don't know. I just wasn't feeling a connection. I can't explain it."

Rhonda pushed a hand through her mane of jet-black hair. In his opinion, many women couldn't pull off bangs, but she was one of the few who could.

"She said you seemed reluctant to even kiss her."

"We kissed," Truman said in his own defense.

"Not like she wanted to, apparently."

"Well, after working all week, I'm tired. I'm not a horny teenager anymore, Rhonda."

She gasped quietly, her eyes opening wide. "Is that what

it is? Do you have a problem?" she asked in a whisper. "Down there?" She pointed one finger downward. "Doctors can do things for that nowadays, Truman."

"What? No." Truman shook his head. "Jesus, Rhonda. No. That's not it at all."

"There's nothing to be ashamed of."

"There's nothing wrong with…things. Okay? Damn." Truman looked around again, making sure no one was listening.

"So, what is it? You're fifty now, you know. There's not a lot of women in the dating pool, especially around here."

"I told you. I just didn't feel a spark. To be honest, it was kinda like dating my sister."

"You don't have a sister," Rhonda said with a smirk. "Besides, this is Alabama. Desperate times call for desperate measures, Truman."

Truman watched her laugh, shaking his head. "Who says I'm desperate? Besides, shouldn't y'all be getting ready for the sequester?"

"Oh no. Don't you try to change the subject, mister. The hubs has it under control. Besides, I called in an order to go." She spared a quick look at the counter, then leaned in over the table. "Look. Tiffany would be a catch for any man your age."

"My age?"

Rhonda shrugged. "You just said you're not a horny teenager anymore." She plucked a fry from his plate and munched on it while she thought. "Tif said she practically threw herself at you on y'all's last date."

Truman shrugged one shoulder, dropping his eyes to his glass.

"Did you know she didn't even wear any panties? You were this close to getting lucky," she held up her thumb and finger, holding them an inch apart. "And you didn't even make a move."

"Look, I don't know what to tell you. Would you rather I slept with her and then broke things off?"

Rhonda chuckled. "She might have. She said she hadn't been laid in months."

"Well…"

"I figured you'd be all over her. I mean, she's got some big boobs and a nice thick booty. Hell, with her blonde hair, she's practically a real-life Barbie doll."

"Maybe I don't go for the Barbie doll type."

"What man doesn't go for the Barbie Doll type, if only for a few romps in the hay?"

"Apparently me." Truman pushed the half-eaten burger toward the edge of the table and motioned to the waitress for his check.

"Just what is your type, Truman?"

"I don't know. I don't even know if I have a type."

"Maybe your type is exotic redheads who ignore you most of the time."

"That's a shitty thing to say."

"I'm sorry." Rhonda plucked another fry from the plate before the waitress could take it away. "I know you two have an on-again, off-again thing going on."

"You do, do you?"

"I hear things, Truman. Just whispers here and there."

"Whispers?" Truman rolled his eyes.

"Yes, whispers. You know how people gossip. This is a small town. People talk, Truman. The lingering glances, the hidden smiles. You two aren't as sly as you think."

"Okay then, let people talk. I don't care."

"Look, we go way back, so I'm gonna be honest with you."

"And you haven't been?" Truman chuckled. He'd known Rhonda and her husband, Trent, almost as long as he'd been in Friendly.

"You're getting to the age where you need to find someone to settle down with. You're going to need a good woman to set your pills out for you, remember where you leave your reading glasses. Stuff like that. That doesn't happen overnight. You need to start building that relationship now."

"Jesus, Rhonda. I'm fifty. I'm not that old."

"Yet," she said. "But in ten years, you'll be sixty. Ten years after that, you'll be seventy years old, Truman. Seventy."

"I can count too, you know."

"Look," she said, her eyes dropping to the chipped nail polish on her fingertips. "I just worry about you. Living in that hotel room all alone. You can't keep wasting your time pining away for a girl who obviously has no interest in a relationship."

Truman's head snapped up. "Did Tiffany tell you to say that?"

"No. Why?"

"Because she said basically the same thing when I broke things off with her."

"Well, there you have it. I'm not the only one who sees it."

"You don't have anything. Did it ever occur to you that I don't want a relationship? Maybe I don't want a woman fetching my pills and bringing my slippers. You ever think about that? And as far as where I choose to live, have you ever considered that I might like my current accommodations?"

"Because it's close to her?"

"Because I don't have to cut grass or patch the roof. I don't have to pay taxes on the place, paint, or fix the plumbing. And—" he pointed a finger at her— "There's a bar right downstairs if I want to drink."

"Those sound a lot like excuses to me."

"Well, they're not. Perhaps, just perhaps, I like my freedom. You ever consider that?"

"Freedom to do what?" she asked.

"Nothing. Freedom to do nothing if that's what I want to do."

"Truman, are you okay?" Her eyes searched his. "I worry about you since Megan left."

"Really?" he scoffed, shaking his head. "I'm fine. And the divorce has nothing to do with this. It's been ten years. I'm good, trust me."

"I know, but sometimes a man takes longer to work through things like that."

"I'm fine, Rhonda." He nodded emphatically. "I am, but thanks for the concern."

"Are you really?" Rhonda laughed as she patted her chest. "Are you okay in here?"

Truman shared her laugh. "Yes. Inside, outside, every side. I'm fine."

"Well then, I've said my peace. I'll leave you alone." She stood and looked down at him with a smile on her face. "But I will say this. You might have missed some fun with ole Tif. Trent knows a guy who went out with her last weekend, and he said she was wild as hell in the sack."

"That might have been good to know beforehand," Truman said, stroking his chin comically. "Anyway, she doesn't seem too broken up about me."

"What can I tell ya? You snooze, you lose, buddy." Rhonda turned and sauntered to the counter, giving the cashier her name. When she brought the order to the counter in a brown paper bag, Rhonda took it and turned back to Truman. "Don't be a stranger. You're looking a little worn out and thin. Come by and have supper with us. I'll make spaghetti. Trent made some beer that he's very proud of. We'll all get drunk, and you can sleep on the couch."

"I will," Truman promised.

She walked back to his table and bent toward him with

a sly grin. Laying a hand alongside her mouth, she whispered, "Then maybe you should get your girlfriend to sew your button back on."

Truman smoothed the front of his shirt. Why was everyone so interested in his damned button?

As he watched her leave, he caught sight of another man doing the same. Sitting at the counter, the man leaned back, his eyes trained on the tight blue jean cut-off shorts Rhonda wore and the long, tanned legs that grew out of them. Though they were old friends, Truman wasn't blind to the fact that Rhonda had a full, round butt that looked great in a pair of shorts.

Truman chuckled as he stood, grabbing his check. He paid the bill, left a generous tip, and then exited the building just in time to see Rhonda's Mustang make the light on Eighth Street and turn right as she headed home.

He sighed, admitting to himself that she was at least partially right. Andrea Ardelean was a lot of things, but she wasn't the button sewing-on type.

CHAPTER SIX

June 3rd. Mid Afternoon.

Andrea Ardelean pulled the heavy drape back from the window, recoiling slightly as a sliver of sunlight stole into the darkened room. She shielded her eyes with her free hand as she looked down on Main Street.

The town was beginning to calm. The bevy of activity had slowed to a trickle. Across the street, a group of people carried suitcases into an old brick building, disappearing behind boarded-up windows. Most people were already where they were going to be for the next few anxious days. If they weren't, they soon would be.

Her eyes went to the empty spot at the far right of the five slots angled to the curb in front of the hotel. The lines of the open slot were painted red, designating that it was reserved. Every other slot was full, as was the side parking lot around the corner.

She sighed and released the curtain, sinking the room back into shadows. "Yes, Jean," she said, answering his question. "I am fully aware of what today is. How could I forget? The workers brought up the wood earlier." She waved a hand at the four sheets of painted plywood leaning against the wall next to her door.

Turning, she looked at the man across the room. Though

he often dyed his hair black, the lines on his face told his real age. "I'll put it up myself."

"You know, if… someone… sees that it's not up by nightfall, it may arouse suspicion." He looked at her, his bushy eyebrows raised slightly. "And we don't need that."

"I know." Andrea bent and pulled her crop of red hair, still wet from her shower, over her left shoulder. She spared Jean a glance as she drug her fingers through it, removing tangles. "I'll take care of it. I promise."

Jean Ardelean sighed. Sitting in a chair across the room, he rubbed the palms of his hands on the legs of his suit pants. "To be perfectly honest, I'm surprised we've stayed here so long."

Ignoring him, Andrea stood and gathered her mane of hair at the nape of her neck, pulling it through her hands. She moved to the closet and opened the doors. Taking out a red dress, she held it against the front of her bathrobe, inspecting the fabric. After a moment's thought, she hung it back up and took out a black one.

A smile slipped across her lips as she tugged at the hemline, which would fall around mid-thigh on her. Sleeveless and made of a cloth that would contour to her body, the dress would be very revealing.

"Did you hear me?" Jean asked quietly.

"I heard you, Jean." Andrea sighed. "Why do you complain so? I thought you liked it here." She replaced the dress and pulled out a long, green one with billowing silk fabric. She loved the dress but didn't think it was right for the occasion. Still, she pulled the fabric through her hand, smiling at the feel of it.

"I do." He looked around the room, a flat smile coming to his face. "I like this hotel. The architecture reminds me of some of the old places."

"Good," Andrea said, holding the dress to her as she fit it to her body. "Then why bring it up?"

Jean shrugged. "We've been here a long time."

"Um-hmm."

"It's just that we usually—"

"Jean." She looked at him with a flat smile. "You do fret so sometimes."

"It's an old habit that I've grown used to."

Andrea sighed as she hung the dress back in the closet. She closed the doors and crossed the room to Jean. Bending, she cradled his chin in her hand and looked down at him with a wide smile. His eyes looked tired, though he tried to hide it. Even his smile looked old and worn out.

"I do appreciate that you worry so, that's why I love you." She kissed his forehead then stood. "But it's not good for you. It will make you old before your time."

Jean chuckled, watching as Andrea went back to the window. "I am old," he said. "If you haven't noticed. Every morning, I find a new wrinkle on my face and a new ache in my body."

"Don't be so dramatic, Jean." Andrea peeked between the drapes. "It's not very becoming." Finding the parking spot empty again, she turned back to him.

"I might only have a few years left, Andrea."

"Do not talk that way. Not today. Please. You're just tired."

"It's true, my sweet. You have eyes. You must know the truth as well as me."

"I have kept you safe all these years, haven't I?" Her eyes searched his face for the evidence that she'd already seen many times but refused to accept. Deep wrinkles crossed his forehead and nested at the corners of his eyes. His skin had taken on the slight, glossy look of old age and didn't cling to his shape the way it once had.

"That's just it." He dropped his eyes, unable to face her. "I don't want you to. I want to live out what time I have here… here in this hotel."

"Then that is what we will do," she said, throwing him a dismissive wave.

Jean stood and went to her. "How much longer do you think we can stay here?"

"We will stay as long as you like." Andrea took his hands in hers, her thumbs caressing the backs of his hands. "Do not worry, dear. I will take care of you."

"But I do. I worry for me and for you after I'm gone."

Andrea forced a smile. This wasn't the first time Jean had spoken of growing old and dying. The idea was heartbreaking in so many ways, and she couldn't bear the thought.

"I will be fine, and so will you." She released his hands and went back to the window, stealing another peek between the drapes.

"You know it will be almost dusk before he arrives," Jean said quietly.

"I haven't a clue what you're talking about." Andrea left the window and went to the small bar set up in the corner, pouring herself a shot of scotch.

"He is a good man. It would be good for you to have someone after I'm gone."

"Please, stop being so foolish."

"Foolish?" Jean shook his head. "I have eyes, Andrea. I see the way he looks at you." He paused, meeting her gaze. "And the way you look at him."

Andrea laughed. "You're a romantic fool," she said. Crossing to Jean, she put a palm on his cheek. "That is one of the things I love most about you."

Jean put his hand over hers and smiled. "I have been on this Earth far longer than I should have been. I do believe that my time is drawing to a close. This may very well be my last season."

Andrea's eyes narrowed slightly as they scoured his face.

"What would I do without you?"

"You will go on, I'm sure."

Andrea shrugged. "I suppose I would, but I'd be lost without you."

Jean laughed, rising from the chair. "You will be fine. I have come to know that I need you more than you need me."

Andrea shook her head as she sighed. "Let's not discuss this today. Please. The hotel is full, and we must get ready for the sequester."

"Yes, I know." Jean stepped back from Andrea. "It is almost time, isn't it?" He went to the door and opened it. Looking back at Andrea, he found her next to the window again. She was young and beautiful but saddled with a heavy secret that she didn't deserve to have to keep. "Andrea?"

"What is it, Jean?" she asked without looking at him.

"Wear the black dress. You will be beautiful in it. He will love it." Without waiting for a reply, he turned and walked out of the room, closing the door behind him.

Truman released the trigger on the cordless drill as the screw head sank into the plywood. He was careful not to strip it because he'd probably be the one to take the sheets of wood down when this was all over.

"I always hate how dark it makes the house."

Truman turned to see Harriet Swanson approaching with an oil lamp in one hand and a can of Coke in the other. Like most of the old women he'd met, she wore a "house dress" — a thin, short-sleeved, modestly patterned dress that hung loosely about her and ended just above her ankles. Her gray hair was pulled back in a tight knot, her face drawn with worry.

"Thank you, ma'am." Truman took the can and slid it across his forehead before opening it. Close to eighty, Harriet kept her house warmer than he liked.

"You know, since Buddy died, it's just been me. He's been gone almost seven years now. Where does the time go?" She gathered the front of her dress in her right hand as she sat in a well-used recliner, holding the lamp on her lap. "He used to put up the wood every year 'till he got to where he couldn't manage. Bless his soul."

"Yes, ma'am."

"We'd always take the mattress off our bed and haul it in here. He put it on the floor right here," she swept one feeble hand across the floor at her feet. "And he used to sit right here in this very chair with that old Mossberg of his and watch over us all night while we slept."

"He sounds like a good man."

"Oh, he was." She nodded, her eyes going misty. "He always looked out for me and the children," she went on, pronouncing it "chirren". "The cancer got him, you know."

"Yes, ma'am. I remember."

"In the end, he was weak as a lamb, but he kept hanging on. One of the nurses said that I should give him permission to go, so I did. He left us the next day."

"I'm sorry for your loss. I'm sure it was a hard thing to do."

She nodded, lost in thought. "The young'uns have done moved off. Matthew is in Florida, and Sue moved to Atlanta."

"Yes, ma'am. Well, I'm glad to help any time you need me. One of us will come by afterward and take these boards down and have someone pick them up for you."

"You know, sometimes I wonder why I even bother. I mean to say, I'm just one old woman. What difference would it make? Maybe taking me would spare someone else. Someone younger."

"Now, don't talk like that, ma'am. You know everybody in town would miss you. Why the cakewalk at the fall festival wouldn't be the same without your blueberry pies."

"Oh, stop," she said, giving him a dismissive wave as a smile spread across her thin lips.

Truman watched the flame flicker inside the glass bell of the lamp as it wobbled on her lap. "You know, I have a new battery lamp in the car if you'd like it. They're a lot safer than those old oil lamps. They put out a lot more light, too."

"Oh, I don't want to be a bother. We've been making it all these years with these old things. I reckon I can make it a few more."

"It's no bother, really. The city bought a ton of them for that very purpose." It wasn't true, but the last thing he wanted was for her to burn herself alive in a house fire. "When I'm done here, I'll bring it in. Maybe you can sit those around and just carry the battery lamp around when you move about." He looked around the dim room. "They're a lot safer too."

"Alright then. If it's no bother. I like to read my bible, and these old eyes aren't what they used to be."

"It's no bother at all." Truman slid the couch back into place in front of her front room window, taking time to straighten the Afghan—a throw woven with brown, yellow, and orange yarn—that hung over the back. He then moved the end table back, careful not to knock over the black-and-white photo of a skinny kid in an army uniform.

"That's my Buddy, there," she said, extending a scrawny finger toward the picture. "He was in the service for nigh twenty years. He started calling on me a month before he left for the Army. We got married one weekend when he was home on leave."

"Handsome fella," Truman said, gathering loose screws from the table.

"We never had a lot, but neither of us minded that too much. We did get to travel some, different bases, and such."

"That sounds interesting."

"I didn't really care for it much. I've always been a homebody, you know. I liked being with him, so I went where he went when I could."

"Well, that's all that matters, right? Being together."

"For me, it t'was."

"Well, I'll get that lamp for—"

"My kids hadn't been back home in nearly a year when he died. They came to the funeral, of course. They stayed for a few days and helped me get things sorted out. Paperwork and whatnot, you know. Then they left. I haven't seen them but Christmastime since."

"I'm sorry to hear that. That's not good," Truman said, not knowing what else to say.

"Oh, they call all the time. They even got me one of them fancy cell phones so we could see each other when we talk. I don't know how to use it. I just keep it charged and hit the button when one of them calls."

"That sounds nice," Truman said and downed another swallow of Coke. "I really need to—"

"I don't mean to make them out to be bad kids. They ain't. They just have busy lives, you know. I got me five grand babies between them."

"That is impressive." Truman inched toward the door.

"Both of them told me they didn't want to bring up their little ones in a town like this. You know what I mean?"

"Yes, ma'am. I can't say that I blame them." Truman grabbed the doorknob, but she kept talking.

"You got any young'uns, officer?"

"No, ma'am. I was married, but we never got around to kids."

"There's still time."

"Well, we're divorced now, so…"

"Oh." She nodded. "Seems like I remember that. You married that Armstrong girl, didn't you?"

"Yes, ma'am. Megan."

She nodded slowly. "Well, a nice-looking man like you with a good, steady job should be able to find a good woman to settle down with."

A flat smile came to Truman's lips. "I guess I'm waiting on the right one to come along."

"Well, don't wait too long. Time only moves one way, you know."

"Yes, ma'am." He reached for the doorknob again, but she continued talking.

"You know. It's hard to believe we've been spared all these years. Buddy said if he'd seen it, he'd have killed it, and I believe him."

"Well, ma'am, no offense, but it was probably best you didn't see it."

"Oh," she sighed. "You're probably right." Her shoulders slumped, allowing the lamp to tilt in her lap.

Truman gasped quietly and moved to her as the red liquid in the glass reservoir sloshed to one side. "Let me get that for you." He took the lamp and sat it on the coffee table. "I'm going to get you that battery lamp. Okay?"

Without waiting for a response, he hurried to the door and ducked through. Though hot, the air outside was a pleasant respite from the stuffy, close air in the house.

On the porch, he squinted in the bright June sunshine and tugged at the neck of his uniform shirt, already showing a dark sweat stain after only being in the house for forty-five minutes. He downed the rest of his soda and sat the can on the banister.

He cast an eye towards the western sky as he walked to his patrol car. The shadows of the trees in Mrs. Swanson's yard were long. The day was coming to a close, and he still had to board up her front door.

He opened the trunk and grabbed the battery lamp. When he closed it, he found her standing on the porch. Her bony hands were clasped in a fist at her chest, and she was staring straight at him. With her hair pulled back in a tight bun, she reminded him of the old woman in the American Gothic painting.

"I reckon this'll be my last breath of fresh air for a few days."

"Unfortunately," he said, walking back to the porch. "You do have air conditioning, don't you?"

She nodded slightly as if lost in thought. "I do, but I keep it set high. That cold air hurts my bones something fierce." She rubbed her bony wrist for emphasis. "Some folks keep it feeling like wintertime. Why, I was down at the grocery store the other day and nearly froze to death. I'm going to have to take to wearing a sweater in there."

"Yes, ma'am." Truman rejoined her on the porch and motioned toward the open front door, but she didn't move.

"You know, we used to talk about what it was. Buddy and me, I mean," she began. Truman nodded patiently, knowing what "it" she was talking about. "Never in front of the little ones, mind you."

"No sense frightening them about it," Truman said, stepping inside to place the lamp by the door and retrieve his drill.

"Oh, I don't think we was ever really scared. Buddy had a way of quelling our fears, you know."

"Yes, ma'am," Truman said, thinking that they were stupid not to be scared. He watched the woman stare at the boarded-up windows of the house across the street. Her eyes seemed larger as the afternoon sun highlighted the gauntness of her face. Her big eyes moved from window to window, absorbing the reason for the plywood's presence.

"Are you okay?"

A pained smile came to her face. "Oh, I'm sure I'll be fine."

"Because there's still time to go somewhere if you're feeling bad or something. The clinic, the school."

She drew in a deep breath and let it out as she shook her head. Finally, she turned to him, meeting his eyes. "You wanna know what we figured it was?" she asked, ignoring his offer. Taking hold of the post next to her, she laid her head against it.

"What, what is?"

"The creature," she said.

Truman shrugged. The last thing he wanted was another citizen's opinion of what the creature was.

"A man."

"A man?" Truman asked, moving closer to the sheet of plywood standing next to the open doorway.

"Yep. A man. Buddy always said a man's the only one who could be so meticulous and so evil to do what was done to all them folks. If it was a bear or cougar or something, it wouldn't tear them up so bad."

"Well, no one really knows for sure what it is, ma'am."

She leveled her gaze at him again, standing with her back straight and her chin up. "It's a man, alright. Trust you me. It's a man."

Truman stared into her eyes, absorbing years of pain and loss as well as the stubborn conviction she felt. He was the proxy for the entire city, bearing the blame for her children moving away. For not being able to see her grandchildren in her golden years. For having to shuffle around an old, dark house alone for three days every June.

When he finally dropped his gaze, she moved into the house with an unsteady gait. "It's a man," she said again as she passed. Once inside, her eyes locked on his as she began slowly pushing the door closed. "The only thing we could never figure out is which one it is."

Truman stared at her until the door shut completely. The click of the deadbolt sliding into place sounded like a gunshot in the silence that hung on the porch.

Shaking off the woman's final words, he slid the sheet of three-quarter-inch thick plywood over her door and began screwing it to the frame, effectively securing the old woman inside her own home.

When he finished, he knocked on the plywood and yelled, "I'm done, ma'am. I'll send someone as soon as I can when it's over."

He waited for a reply, but none came. Turning with a groan, he jogged down the steps and went to his car. Tossing the drill into the passenger seat, he climbed behind the wheel and started the car, sighing with relief as the first cold wind of the air conditioner washed over him.

CHAPTER SEVEN

June 3rd. Dusk

Truman released a long, low grunt as he turned the corner onto 4th Street and saw the First Presbyterian Church. Floodlights shone from each corner of the building, illuminating the lush landscaping that surrounded it. The four stained glass windows on the side he could see, each one of them close to ten feet tall, glowed like beacons in the gathering twilight.

Unwilling to deprive people of air conditioning in the June heat, the city didn't turn off the power. Most people willingly accepted the "dark and quiet" guidelines. No one was sure if it made much difference, but common sense seemed to dictate that it did.

The brakes on his cruiser squeaked as he rolled up to the curb in front of the church, alerting the two men standing on the porch of the church of his presence. They looked at him, then at each other. When he got out of the car, they watched him walk up the sidewalk, moving to meet him at the top of the steps.

"Evening, gentlemen," Truman said, offering a smile.

"Truman." The taller of the men, Lester Howard, gave him a nod.

"Got 'er lit up tonight. Don't you?"

The shorter man that Truman vaguely remembered stayed

quiet while Lester spoke up defiantly. "Yup."

Truman nodded. "Do you think that's a good idea?"

Lester shrugged. "I don't know if it is or it ain't, but the preacher decided to take a stand, and I agree with him."

"Take a stand against what, exactly?" Truman asked.

"Fear, hiding, whatever you want to call it."

Truman drew in a deep breath, nodding as he looked around the porch. His eyes met the shorter man's, and he looked away. "As you know, Lester, there's no city ordinance against it, but—"

"Then why are you here?" He swallowed, and his voice lost some of its edge. "If you don't mind my asking."

Truman shrugged. "I guess I was hoping to talk some sense into y'all. There are lots of folks who seek shelter here. Maybe they don't want all the attention."

"We got plenty of room in the basement. Those with concerns are down there."

"That's good."

"Truman, you know me. I ain't got a beef with you or nobody else. Sometimes you just got to trust in the Lord and let him demonstrate his power."

"I'm not arguing that fact with you, Lester. But the good Lord also gave us common sense. I figure he expects us to use that, too."

"Well, you're more than welcome to stay with us. Bunch of us are going to be sitting in a prayer vigil with the preacher."

Truman took a step back down the steps. "I appreciate it, Lester. Give Reverend Dower my apologies for missing, but I'm the law presence over at the Jupiter."

"We'll put in a word for you, Truman."

"I appreciate it. You fellas have a good night."

"We'll be in the presence of the Lord. That's always a good night."

"Let's hope so." Truman started down the sidewalk but stopped and turned around. "Has there ever been an attack here before?"

"Not that I know of. No demon would dare come into the Lord's house."

Truman nodded. "Maybe you're right. Maybe it just avoids big crowds."

"Either way," Lester said, shrugging one shoulder.

"Well, I won't keep you. Curfew starts at dusk, gentlemen. There *is* a city ordinance about that." Truman gave them a curt nod and started for his car again.

"Officer?" Truman turned back to the men as the shorter of them finally found his voice. "Don't you trust God to protect you? Do you think this thing is stronger than God Almighty?"

"No sir, I don't. That's not it at all."

"Then what is it?" Lester asked.

Truman sighed, collecting his thoughts. "Well, I've seen firsthand what this thing can do, and all I know is that I'd like more between me and it than a thin piece of colored glass."

"Ain't got nothing to do with the windows, Truman. It's the power of the Lord that stands between us and it."

Truman nodded, then turned his eyes toward the west. The red and orange sky had given way to a pale lavender color that reminded him of an old bruise. The day was practically gone. He drew in a deep breath and exhaled slowly before turning back to the men.

"Well, I can't say for sure, Lester, but I imagine when folks know this thing is outside their house, they go to praying harder than hell. It didn't seem to help them." He turned and walked toward the street.

He was almost to his car when someone called after him. He stopped, shaking his head. Turning slowly, he watched the second man hurry down the steps and along the sidewalk toward him.

"Look, uh, my name is John Cramer. I'm not from here. I mean, I've lived here a long time, but I wasn't born here, you know?"

"Okay," Truman said.

"Well, is it true that most of the people who this thing comes after are not born here? Like we're outsiders or something."

Truman drew in a deep breath and let it out slowly. "I don't think so."

"But I was talking to Bert Peterson down at the feed store the other day—"

"Look, Mister Cramer, as best anyone can tell, there is no rhyme or reason to the attacks. Some folks are lucky, some aren't. That's all it is."

The man rubbed his mouth with the palm of his hand and spared Lester a glance as he waited on the porch. "I don't mean to imply nothing, but some folks are starting to talk about what this thing might be. Lotta folks are saying it's a vampire—"

Truman held up his hand, stopping the man. "No one has any proof of what it is, sir. Anything anyone says is pure speculation."

"But what if it is? That'd mean it's someone in town."

Truman sighed and looked at the failing light in the west. "It's almost dark. Maybe you should get inside." Truman opened his car door and turned back to the man. "And do yourself a favor. Stop listening to gossip."

Truman Malone pulled into the last remaining spot in front of the Jupiter Hotel. Turning off the engine, he sat in his thirteen-year-old police cruiser, staring through the windshield at the only building he'd ever felt genuine affection for.

The hotel, built in a time when craftsmanship and style took precedence over profit margins, was more suited for a town like Charleston or New Orleans. In Friendly, Alabama, the Jupiter Hotel was a beautiful girl standing among wallflowers.

What Rhonda had called "that old hotel" felt as much like home to him as any place he'd ever lived. There was a romance to it that seemed lost on everyone else in town. To him, it was like being in the presence of royalty. It was more than just a building. It represented a grandeur, an elegance that was all but lost nowadays.

A pair of fluted columns guarded each of the front corners of the hotel. Climbing the full height of the building and ending in massive decorative capitals, they lent the place a look of stately sophistication. The fact that they were showing their age added to their charm.

Centered on the columns was a set of doors that commanded attention. Standing nine feet tall, the doors were made of dark, rich wood that had weathered well. Three concentric circles of carved wood sat at the center of each door, surrounded by intricately carved panels, creating a square frame around them. The lower half of the door repeated the corner pattern, but the center shape was a single wooden diamond.

Sitting atop the doors was an arched transom, the antique wavy glass resting behind ornate, cast metal fingers that protruded from the frame that held it in place.

The doors gave way to a facade of tumbled bricks that had been painted. Harkening to a bygone era, the pale green color, neither garish nor subdued, fit the place perfectly.

Above the doors, two rows of arched windows looked out over Main Street, the sill of each a single slab of natural stone. Dental work, left in a natural state to match the windowsills, rimmed the top of the building like a crown atop the head of a regal queen.

Higher still, growing from the roof, a wooden framework supported a silent neon sign that spelled out Jupiter Hotel in large script letters. Silhouetted against the approaching twilight, the cold, dead neon tubes barely resembled the iconic structure that usually dominated downtown. Seeing the massive sign dark sent a pang of sadness through his chest that he couldn't quite come to terms with.

The hotel was equipped with generators in the event of a power failure, so the absence of the purple and green tubes of light was conspicuous. Nothing else in town stood as stark a reminder of the date as the dark Jupiter Hotel sign.

Above the hotel, the dying sun threw out its last spears of light, painting the bottom of the gathering clouds with a strange orange glow. Silhouetted against this sky, the sign took on a foreboding glow. Truman dropped his gaze quickly. The date and the things that would happen were bad enough. He didn't want to add this image to those that already haunted him.

There were things that seemed trivial to one man yet tore at the soul of another. Seeing the hotel like this was one of those things for Truman. To him, it was like hearing a dark secret about an old friend or realizing that a love affair was coming to an end. The established order of things was going with the setting sun, and, once again, the sequester was beginning.

He rubbed his face with both hands and sighed through them. His affinity for the hotel went further than a passing appreciation for architecture. It was personal. He first came here after his divorce. He'd lost his wife, his home, and the future he had planned. Broken, both spiritually and financially, the Jupiter Hotel was where he'd rebuilt himself, renewed his spirit, and found a new purpose.

In time, he grew to like the staff and the charm of the place enough to stay. Room 307 had been his home for the past ten years, and he had no plans to leave anytime soon. Contrary to what his friend believed, living here suited him. When he wanted alone time, he could go to his room. When he wanted to be around people, he could go to the bar or the dining room.

The romantic in him saw himself as the de facto hotel detective, like in the old movies. Any time something happened, they called him. Not the station. Him.

He had a nice, quiet spot on the corner of the third-floor. For most of the year, the back windows in his room looked over a vacant lot between the Bank and Trust and The Wild, a small restaurant specializing in wild game meats. Sometimes, he watched the neighborhood kids play a pickup game of basketball or something that they called wall ball. He'd also caught more than one kid trying to sneak a smoke or share a bottle of beer with his friends. In those cases, he'd just yell down to them, and, having been seen, they'd scurry away to find another hideout.

Unfortunately, like every window of every other occupied dwelling in town, his windows were boarded up.

His eyes swept up the building, landing on one group of windows. Andrea Ardelean's room possessed the last two windows on the front left-hand side of the building and the first two on the side.

A smile snuck across his lips as he thought of her, wondering if she were in her room. With all the preparations for the sequester, they'd both been busy. Until this morning, but even that didn't end the way he wanted.

He'd noticed that as the time drew closer and closer every year, he saw less and less of her. Of course, this wasn't completely out of the ordinary, even when the sequester wasn't looming. Like most people, she avoided the subject. He'd never brought it up to her, assuming that, like everyone else in town, she had her own way of dealing with the event.

Though some people seemed to take the sequester in stride, he couldn't see how anyone couldn't be profoundly impacted by it. Even if you never lost anyone close to you, just the fact that it was happening and could happen to you surely affected people's psyche in one way or another. Andrea was no different.

Besides, it wasn't like he and Andrea were an official couple or anything. To be honest, he didn't know what they were.

Lost in thought, Truman jumped when a knock came suddenly on the glass next to his head. Looking around, he saw the smiling face of a tall man with broad shoulders and a comb-over that didn't work as well as he thought it did. Benjamin Steely. Truman groaned internally as he rolled down the window. He didn't like anything about the man, but his position required at least a modicum of civility.

"Kinda jumpy, ain't we?" the man asked, a smile tugging at the corners of his mouth.

"Lockdown started half an hour ago, Ben."

"I know. Just picking up a few last-minute necessities." Ben reached into the bag clutched under his left arm and revealed the neck of a liquor bottle. "The Loopers are coming this year, and they like the good stuff. It was late coming in at the package store."

Truman stared at the man, unimpressed. "Who are the Loopers?"

"They're big real estate developers from up around Souls Harbor. Potential investors."

Truman rolled his window back up and got out of the car. Now wearing jeans and a tee shirt, he shoved his hands into his pockets and shook his head, taking a deep breath to calm himself. Ben's big dream was to build a waterpark on sixty acres of farmland just outside of town that he'd bought cheap after the family was killed six years earlier. He'd approached the city several times about permits and tax breaks and pretty much never shut up about his "big plan."

"You brought in out-of-towners? Today? Are you out of your mind?"

"Oh, settle down," Ben replied with a dismissive wave.

"We'll be inside the whole time. They loved the idea of being shut in for three days. Some people have busy schedules and enjoy a break every now and then. Plus, it gives me a captive audience, so to speak." He laughed, pleased with his own joke.

"You know the chief is going to be pissed."

"Oh, the chief can get over it. I talked to the mayor about it, and he's fine with it."

"He would be," Truman scoffed.

"You worry too much, Truman. You should relax some. Stress will make you old before your time, you know. It's a silent killer."

Truman rubbed his eyes with his fingertips, dragging his hands down his face with a frustrated moan. "Look, Ben, don't you think you're being awfully nonchalant about all this? I mean, come on man. Some of your neighbors will die."

"It's going to happen whether I worry about it or not. Besides, most of 'em wouldn't care if it happened to me. I say make the most of it, silk purse and a sow's ear and all that." He waved his hand between them. "And if I can convince the Loopers to invest, so much the better."

"Well, the Loopers and everyone else should already be where they're going to be. And so should you."

"I know. Jesus, man. They're all getting settled in. I had to run one errand. I'm headed in now. I just have to cross the street, you know."

"Then cross it and get inside." The man looked at him defiantly, but Truman's silent glare broke his resolve. When Ben finally gave up and turned, Truman watched until he was across the street.

His eyes drifted to the two-story brick building that still wore the faded paint declaring it Anderson's Hardware. Ben had bought it and turned it into his office/fun house. Though he'd never been invited in, the word was that there were four apartments upstairs while the downstairs served as a private bar equipped with a restaurant-quality kitchen.

The outside of the large plate glass storefront windows was covered with sheets of plywood that had been painted black.

"You're supposed to board up the windows on the inside, Ben."

"I did." He waved a hand at the sheets of plywood as he passed them. "I'm tired of bumping around in the dark, for goodness' sake. This year, we're going to light it up, and I figured we'd need the extra protection."

Truman shook his head. While most people in town hunkered down, Benjamin Steely always threw a lavish party. He invited the top socialites in town, and the word was that they wined and dined for three days. Some rumors mentioned huge orgies, but that was probably just bitterness from the people who didn't get invited. Either way, having a party while people hid under the specter of a gruesome death hardly seemed right, but there was nothing he could do about it.

Truman shook his head as Ben disappeared into the building across the street, some of his disdain for the man fading. Hell, he was just surviving like the rest of them.

People used any number of things to distract themselves during the sequester, the main thing being alcohol. A few days before the curfew kicked in, you'd begin to see people at the package store stocking up. Even if they weren't regular drinkers, they drank during the sequester. Things being what they were, people needed something to take the edge off. Luckily, the fine people of Friendly had the tact not to mention who they saw there or how much they were buying, at least not in public.

Another thing was puzzles. Lots of people did puzzles. Putting together a puzzle was a good way to while away the hours. It didn't take much light or effort, and it was quiet. The Jupiter used to provide a massive thousand-piece puzzle every year for its guests.

They were always pictures of beautiful gardens with plenty of colorful flowers or countrysides with fields of wildflowers. A special table was set up in the center of the dining room, encouraging people to come together. He himself had slipped a piece or two into place through the years, even though he hated doing puzzles. When people began choosing to drink in the bar instead of toiling over the tiny pieces, they gave it up.

Other people binge-watched movies in their basements. Some worked on their hobbies, and some caught up on their sleep. Some folks found other things to do to keep busy.

Early March, nine months after the sequester, was a big time for new births. There were always one or two "sequester babies," but one year, there had been six. Three people had died that year, making a net positive for the town.

Three days was a long time to stay cooped up, no matter what you did. Luckily, he had everything he needed right here at the hotel.

He sighed and spared one last glance at the darkening sky before turning and walking into the Jupiter.

CHAPTER EIGHT

June 3rd. Sunset

The extravagance of the lobby couldn't be hidden by the scant light of the lamps arranged along the walls. The lamps rested on five-foot Roman-style pillars in a space normally occupied by luxurious ferns.

The dream of a local recluse who'd died long before Truman came to town, the building was a labor of love. To him, the whole place was a work of art, and the lobby was at its heart.

Corinthian marble floors swept beneath a massive chandelier that hung from the ceiling three floors up. The flickering, yellow flames of the lamps danced within the countless pieces of crystal, stirred slightly by the door closing behind him. As tall as a grown man and as big around as a dinner table, the chandelier itself probably cost more than Truman made in a year, but it looked like it was made for the place.

Across the room, a grand staircase dominated the space. Anchored by massive, carved mule posts, it ushered patrons to a wide landing on the second-floor. That, in turn, led to hallways on each side of the hotel. A dark green carpet, delicately patterned in gold, ran up the center of the steps, held to the back of each tread with a brass bar.

On the right side of the landing, a smaller staircase hugged the wall, coming back toward the front of the hotel, serving the few rooms on the third-floor. Its polished wooden belly glimmered in the faint light.

To the left of the staircase, there was a small concierge's counter, giving way to a hallway that served the rooms on the main floor.

Just as it was on the exterior, the craftsmanship and design of the interior were mostly lost on the locals. People either passed between the rich mahogany doors on the left of the lobby en route to the bar or between a matching set on the right and went to the restaurant. Few ever bothered to pause long enough to appreciate the grandeur of the place. But then again, Friendly wasn't exactly a mecca of architectural design.

Friendly, Alabama, was a small town full of simple people who struggled to make it to the end of the week with a couple of dollars left. Few of them ever stayed in the hotel. Those who did only did so on special occasions like weddings or anniversaries.

"Oh, thank goodness. We were getting worried," came a voice that Truman knew as well as his own father's. Though he'd lived in Friendly for years, the Slavic accent was still thick in Jean Ardelean's voice, especially when he was upset. Like everyone else in town, Jean was upset tonight.

Truman turned to the tall, thin man approaching him from the consigner's station. He wore his age better in his hair than on his face, leading Truman to wonder if his head full of black hair was dyed. Normally neatly kept, Jean's hair was a mess, a sign of his worry and business. Wearing his ever-present dark suit and tie, he stopped just short of Truman and sighed.

"Hi, Jean. Everything okay?"

The man's broad face erupted with a smile. "Now it is. It is getting late. I was concerned for you. I was beginning to wonder if you found another place to stay this year." The man pushed a hand through his hair and cast his eyes to the sheets of plywood standing against the wall.

"You were concerned?" Truman asked with a smile. "That's good to know. What about Andrea?"

"Yes, yes," Jean said, waving a hand dismissively. "I'm sure she was worried too."

Truman's smile turned into a sly grin as he wondered how closely Jean Ardelean watched what his daughter did. Usually, he was back at the hotel much earlier, leaving him to wonder if it was Andrea who worried about where he was staying. "Why would I find another place to stay, Jean?" Truman asked. "I live here, remember?"

"I don't know. Andrea says I worry too much." Jean rubbed his left temple. "We've made all the necessary preparations. Lots of guests. Lots to do, you know. And you are late, so we couldn't finish the doors."

"I'm sorry. I got tied up helping Mrs. Swanson with her windows. She's old and doesn't have anyone else."

"Such a nice man." Jean put a hand on Truman's cheek, patting it gently. "Come," he said, ushering him past the opened doors and into the crowded lounge. A lamp flickered on each of the tables, fending off the darkness with tiny pools of light.

"Intimate," Truman said with a smile. "You should do this more often." His eyes swept up to the two miniature versions of the chandelier in the lobby. Usually, they lit the place in a soft glow, but tonight, they, too, had gone dark.

After instructing two workers to board up the doors, he followed Truman to the bar. "Are you hungry? Andrea made lots of sandwiches. We also have a cold soup, but it's an old family recipe. You may not like it."

"Maybe later. Thanks."

"A drink then?" Jean asked, motioning to the bartender, a stocky man with a bald head and bushy beard. Truman knew his name was Gregg but little else about him.

"Now that, I'll take you up on. It's been a long day."

"Good. Good. You relax. I have work to do still." Jean scurried away, leaving him to the bartender and the other patrons seeking shelter in the Jupiter's lounge. In Friendly, during the sequester, people who felt that their homes didn't provide adequate shelter congregated in one of four places in town.

One was the First Presbyterian Church. For those who liked their sequester with less praying and psalm singing, there was the local high school. They slept on cots and ate sandwiches, but like the church, it was free. Some years, their numbers swelled to two hundred souls.

Another place was the basement of City Hall. Mostly reserved for city workers and their families, they usually housed fifty or so people.

The Jupiter Hotel was the last one, but you had to rent a room. Some people thought it rude that Jean made money off people's fear, but the hotel wasn't that expensive, and they did foot the bill for boarding the windows, providing meals, and cleaning the place back up afterward. Everyone else who didn't get an invitation to Ben's party stayed home and rode it out by themselves.

Picking up his bourbon and coke, Truman turned on his stool and surveyed the lounge. It was rarely this full, but people were taking the edge off. Every year at this time, the whole town started to get wound tighter than a clock.

People's names for the three days in June were as varied as the way they passed them. The Sequester was the official name for it, but there was also The Big Hide, The Dark Days, Devil Days, and The June Swoon. Truman just thought of it as "that time of year." Giving it a slick name never sat well with him.

As one of the four police officers in town, not counting the Chief, he was tasked with keeping the peace at the hotel as best he could. Hopelessly outnumbered, he gave people a long leash during this time. Knowing most of the people and their temperaments helped tremendously. Luckily, there weren't many people in town who caused enough trouble to be memorable.

As he scanned the faces, relief slowly crept into his chest. No one in tonight's crowd raised any red flags except maybe Tommy Ledbetter. Tommy was a big guy who owned a farm outside of town. His wife had left him a few years back and taken his two sons, leaving him to manage the farm alone. He could get mean when he drank hard liquor, which was the reason for his divorce. Luckily, tonight, he was having a beer with Mark Washburn and Andy Jones. Those two never caused any real trouble, so they'd probably keep Tommy in line.

Truman sipped his drink and wiped his mouth with the back of his hand. That was good. He needed a quiet night. The build-up to these three days had been worse than usual. He'd been through twenty-three sequesters, and this year was the most stressful. He couldn't put a feeling on it, but something had his stomach in knots for weeks.

There was also a nagging suspicion in the back of his mind that this year would be a bad one in terms of the body count. He'd been fighting the notion by telling himself it was because he'd just turned fifty. He didn't believe it, but he couldn't figure out a better reason.

He was about to turn back to the bar when a small group stepped into the doorway of the lounge. They stopped, surveying the room. The man said something to his wife, and a quiet but animated discussion broke out. Finally, she turned away and took the two children, a boy and a girl who looked to be around ten, across the lobby to the dining room. Truman's stomach clenched as he watched the man weave his way across the room toward him. He'd never seen the man before. That meant, including the Loopers, there were at least six out-of-towners that had to be kept on a short leash.

"Hi there," Truman said, forcing a smile as the man settled into the stool next to him. "Truman Malone." Truman shook the man's hand. "Nice to meet you. I'm a police officer here in town." When the man's eyes dropped to the drink in Truman's hand, he added, "I'm off duty."

"Brandon Collins."

Truman watched the stranger order a double scotch on the rocks. He was thin, with short blonde hair swept to one side. His yellow Polo was tucked neatly into his khaki shorts. Truman pegged him for a man who drove an expensive car but never looked under the hood.

"New in town?" he asked.

The man shook his head, chuckling as if the idea were preposterous. "Just passing through, actually. Car trouble."

"Ah." Truman nodded and sipped his drink. He was right.

The man paid for his drink with a ten-dollar bill and turned back to Truman. "I have to say, I'm not sure I really understand all of this." He waved his free hand around the bar. "It's just blowing me away."

"Didn't they explain it to you?"

"The tow truck driver said something about a shelter in place order. I don't know." The man sipped his drink and then shook his head again. "I don't get it."

Truman nodded. The story was a cover made up years ago in case any out-of-towners were present when June third rolled around. It hadn't happened often, but there had been a few through the years.

"There's a military arsenal up the road a piece. Sometimes, they destroy weapons-grade ammunition. Bombs and stuff, I guess. I don't really know myself. It's all hush-hush. Federal stuff, you know. Anyway, when they do their thing, we get to shelter in place the day before, the day of, and the day after in case there's a breach or something."

"Rather inconvenient, wouldn't you say?"

Truman shrugged and swirled the drink in his hand, watching the stranger survey the crowd. "What are you gonna do, you know? It's the Feds."

The man shook his head again as he turned toward Truman. "Well, y'all might not mind it, but it's really screwed our timeline up. We were supposed to check into our condo at the beach tonight." He tapped his fingertip on the bar for emphasis.

"That is unfortunate. A bit of bad luck, I guess, huh?"

"You could say that. I should have stayed on the interstate." The man turned his back to the bar and sipped his drink. "But why all this? Boarding up windows and shutting off the electricity? That seems excessive."

"I'm sorry. I just do what I'm told. I think it's in case there's an explosion, maybe. Or a gas leak."

"Hell of a place to put a town."

"I think the town was here first."

The man shrugged and sipped his drink. "Still."

"If it's any consolation, the power isn't shut off. The A/C and the hot water still work."

"That's something, I guess. It's ridiculous if you ask me. Stupid transmission," the man griped, shaking his head.

"Well, look on the bright side. Jimmy will have plenty of free time to work on your car. By the time this is over, your car will be back in shape, and you'll be on your way."

"Jimmy," the man said, rolling his eyes.

Truman laughed. Jimmy Dozer was the only mechanic in town, so the man's car had to be in his shop. Jimmy was a big man who spent most of the summer in a pair of overalls with no shirt underneath. He was country as a cornbread but good at what he did. "Don't let his demeanor fool you. He's really quite the whiz with a vehicle."

"I certainly hope so."

Truman finished his drink and motioned for another. "I'll tell you what. I know the owner here. Since you're just passing through and got caught up in this mess, I'll see if he can waive your room fees."

The man nodded. "That would be nice. God only knows what the car will cost to fix."

"No problem."

The man finished the rest of his drink in one gulp and slid the glass across the bar. "My family is across the way in the restaurant. I better join them, or the wife will be giving me hell all night." The man started off but stopped and turned back to Truman. "Three whole days? Really?"

"They said we'll probably get the all-clear around noon on the fifth."

"Great." He massaged his forehead with one hand. "Anyway, thanks again for the info."

"No problem," Truman said. He sighed as the man walked away, and a knot tightened in his stomach that not even the bourbon could loosen. This was going to be a bad year.

Turning back to the bar, his eyes fell on the rows of liquor bottles sitting on glass shelves inside a wide, open cabinet on the opposite wall. Matching the rest of the hotel's grand style, it, too, was a masterful piece of craftsmanship.

Spanning the full length of the bar, the wood of the cabinet was a soft, caramel color that only came from age and countless layers of tongue oil. At each end, the cabinet fell with a gentle sweeping curve that joined the bar itself. Like the chandelier in the lobby, a year's salary wouldn't come close to the cost of such a beautifully made piece.

Truman took another sip and sat the glass down, thankful for the absence of mirrors behind the bar. He felt tired and probably looked worse. The last thing he wanted to see was the worry on his own face. He'd seen enough worry for a while.

His eyes fell to the glass in his hand. Watching condensation collect on the tumbler, his mind turned back to the aftermath of last year's event. Only two people had died. Lester Champion, an old man who lived on the eastern edge of town, and Lenora Binion, a divorced woman in her late fifties who lived alone with her seven cats.

His boss was right. This thing that came every year was a blight on an otherwise nice town. Everyone got along well, and there were no major issues. Little crime. Old women grew rose bushes, secretly competing for the prize blooms. People tended gardens in their backyards. Most of those who didn't have full-fledged gardens at least had a few tomato plants tucked away in a sunny spot. People hunted in the winter and fished in the summer. They went to work and came home. They raised kids, grilled out, and drank a few beers on the weekend. And once a year, they hid.

The town had a few festivals throughout the year that always enjoyed a large turnout. In so many ways, it was an idyllic small southern town, but this secret hung over everything like a plague.

Like the Mayor, a lot of people in town believed the creature to be a vampire because of the thing with the victim's blood. He did his best to dispel the rumors, but people believed what they wanted. No matter what people thought it was, their fear of it was enough to make them obey the curfew, so ultimately, it didn't matter.

While everyone else remained sheltered, the police and a few volunteers would go out on the fifth of June and find two or three people left like the others. Torn up badly. Bloodless.

They were easy to find because their homes would be torn to hell and back as the creature fought its way in. There was no rhyme or reason to the attacks, but if you wanted to, you could see a pattern, slight as it was.

The one thing that every attack had in common was that there was an older person involved. Sometimes, there were others, but Truman thought them to simply be collateral damage. To his knowledge, there had never been an attack where only young people died. A few times, they'd also found a dog or two killed, but he assumed that to be more self-defense than anything else. The bodies of the dogs were always intact. Their blood was never taken.

They retrieved the bodies, took them to the morgue, and cleaned up the house as best they could. A few days later, there'd be one funeral for all who'd died. Closed caskets. After that, everyone would simply get on with their lives, thankful to have been spared. It was a morbid, twisted tradition that people in Friendly bore as graciously as they could. They took up an offering the following Sunday at church for the families. Whether out of guilt or relief, the people always gave generously. After the funeral and the church services, no one spoke of it again until late May of the following year.

By the Fourth of July, the town would be back to its old self. People acted as if nothing had ever happened. Most years, even the families of the victims came out to join in the celebration.

He sighed and sipped his drink as his boss' words ran through his mind once again. "All we can do is keep as many people as safe as we can and spare their loved ones from seeing them like that. The choices are shit or more shit. That's it. End of story."

Truman agreed one hundred percent. He'd seen the power of this thing. Taking it on would be suicide, plain and simple. Hell, the Marines probably couldn't stop it.

Still, he couldn't completely assuage the guilt that came every year in early June. They were the cops. It was their duty to protect people. The fact that they had no chance in hell of doing it did little to soften the blow.

The first few years he'd endured it, the whole thing knocked him on his ass. It was so surreal. He couldn't understand why they didn't call someone. He came to learn that there was no one to call. No one would ever believe them.

After one particularly bad year, he'd even gone as far as threatening to leave his wife if she didn't move away with him. Being from Friendly, she'd grown up with the specter of the thing and took it all in stride. In the end, she won out, and he stayed. When they divorced, she moved away, and he stayed.

He sighed. "Damn."

"What's that?"

Truman looked up to find Gregg, the bartender, looking at him. "Oh, nothing," he said with a chuckle. "I was just thinking."

Gregg stopped wiping the bar and pointed at him. "This is a bar," he said with a grin. "It's no place for things such as that."

"Gregg, isn't it?" Truman asked with an obligatory laugh.

"The one and only."

"Are you from here?" Truman asked.

"I'd hate to think I was from somewhere else and moved here," Gregg answered, shaking his head.

"That's exactly what I did."

Gregg shook his head. "Then you're entitled to a few 'Damns.'"

"How do you deal with this thing?"

"What? The sequester?" Gregg shrugged. "I don't think about it much, to be honest. It's just one of those things, you know. Anyway, I work nights and sleep all day, so it isn't that big of a change in my routine. The only difference is for the next couple of days, I'll be sleeping here for free. I got me a little single-wide down at Sunrise Park, so the accommodations are an upgrade."

Truman nodded. "You ever lose anybody?"

"Luckily, no. I'm an only child. My folks moved away after they retired. It's just me. No wife and kids or anything like that. How about you?"

Truman shook his head. "I've known a few people, you know, but I don't have any family in town either."

"Seems like that's the way to go."

Truman agreed, lifting his drink. "Well, here's to a safe few days."

"Yeah," Gregg said with a grunt. "It won't be for some poor bastards, I suppose."

Truman watched him walk away, going to another customer down the bar. He was right. People would die. Lives would come to a gruesome, fearful end, and there would be no one to call for help. No one.

CHAPTER NINE

June 3rd. Early Evening

A sandwich wrapped in wax paper plopped onto the bar next to Truman's third drink. A small round sticker with a yellow smiley face held the perfectly creased edges of the paper together in the center.

Dragged from his unpleasant thoughts, Truman's heart rose into his throat, and a smile slipped across his lips. He inhaled the sweet scent of perfume that suddenly washed the air around him, and he shuddered internally, nearly overwhelmed with a sense of joy. He'd been dreading the coming night, but now maybe he wouldn't have to spend it alone.

He gathered himself quickly and looked around to find a beautiful redhead standing next to him. A slender arm extended to the bar, resting one elbow on it while her fingertips twirled a lock of auburn hair. Her lips were painted a deep maroon and were pulled into a coy smile.

Big green eyes sparkled in the dim glow of the oil lamp on the bar as they searched his face urgently. He looked into her eyes, and his breath stopped. His body reacted to her in the way it always did. His heart raced, his stomach knotted, and a fire began to grow in his crotch.

"Well, aren't you a deep thinker?" she asked quietly.

"Not even a little bit," he said, unable to hold back his smile.

"Solving the world's problems?" she asked, one perfectly sculpted eyebrow arching slightly. "Or just getting drunk?"

"Considering that I'm just a small-town cop and I can't even solve small-town problems, I think the world is on its own."

"Then getting drunk it is," she said. Her smile widened as she slid onto the stool next to him. "Want some company?"

"That depends. Is Jean around?"

Andrea smiled. "Is someone still pouting about this morning?"

"Little bit," he said with a chuckle as he turned to her.

His eyes washed over her voluminous crop of auburn hair that hung about her shoulders in big, loose tendrils, and something moved within him. He wanted to get lost in her hair, to have it envelop him. Like the delicate face it framed, her hair was perfect.

His eyes slid to the sleek black dress that clung to her thin but shapely form. His gaze dropped to the toned legs sneaking from the dress, then back up at her eyes. "New dress?" he asked casually, hoping to mask the longing now coursing through his veins.

"Um-hmm," she said with a slight head tilt. "You like it?"

Truman nodded. "Very much so."

Her nose crinkled slightly as she gave him a playful smile. "I thought you might."

Truman's smile grew. It was a new dress. That was a good sign. The dance they danced was usually subtle and reserved, but today, it was different. "What would you have done if I said I was solving the world's problems?"

She plucked the straw from her drink as the bartender delivered it and slid it between her lips, chewing on it slowly as her eyes surveyed him. Finally, she pulled the straw out and absently tossed it onto the bar. "I'd still get drunk. I'd just do it by myself."

Truman laughed. Andrea didn't have her father's accent, but she did possess a throaty, raspy voice that would have sounded sexy reading the farm report. "What's this?" he asked, nodding to the sandwich.

"Papa said you looked hungry. He worries about you. He wants to feed everyone until they are big and fat. He has made a large pot of Ciorba de Potroace." she told him with a shrug.

Truman shrugged, giving her a quizzical look.

"It is a sour soup that we eat cold. Papa's is quite good, but I do not think you would like it."

Truman nodded. "He mentioned that."

"So, I brought you a sandwich. I did go through the trouble of making it just for you."

"Just for me?" Truman said as he carefully unwrapped the sandwich. "A new dress and a personal sandwich. What did I do to get so lucky?"

Andrea put a hand on his shoulder, sending lightning bolts down his spine as she leaned in close. "I know what you like," she whispered. "Besides, you haven't gotten lucky yet, but maybe if you get me drunk enough, you will later on."

Truman inhaled the light, airy scent of her perfume again, letting it saturate his senses. He closed his eyes, allowing her presence and her scent to loosen muscles that he didn't know were tense. His body yearned for hers in ways that he'd never felt, and he wished every moment with her would last an eternity.

He opened his eyes and looked at Andrea, smiling knowingly. In the ten years since his divorce, he and Andrea had gotten together, physically, about a dozen times. Every time was as wonderful as the first. Every touch of her hand still set him afire. Every word sent his mind reeling. Being with her wasn't just companionship or even great sex. It was an event.

Just the sight of her moving throughout the hotel in her duties, made his heart skip a beat. For him, every sighting, every glance, was like catching a glimpse of a rare, exotic bird that he wanted to possess. When she noticed his stare, she'd smile and give him a quick wink. Other times, when she didn't see him, he'd just watch her, enjoying the secret intimacy they shared.

There was a mystery about her that intrigued his mind as much as her body beckoned his own. She refused to reveal her age, but he guessed her to be in her late thirties, judging by her father's age. However, she looked barely out of her twenties, with flawless skin and a long, toned body. A few fine lines had crept in at the corners of her eyes, but that only served to make her sensuality take on a more mature, capable look.

She'd also avoided his attempts to start a proper relationship with her, always saying that her life was "complicated" and that he should "enjoy the time they had together." He'd long since decided not to risk ruining things by badgering her and to accept her affection on her terms.

She did, however, seem to like his company, at least occasionally, and to the best of his knowledge, he was the only man in town who ever got the chance to get close to her. He counted himself lucky to have gotten so far with the most desirable woman in town.

Both Rhonda and Tiffany Jasper had said he was a fool for pining away for something he'd never have. It was an idea that had crossed his mind several times as well, but all it took was one look from Andrea, and all was right with the world. If that made him a fool, then so be it. He'd wait for as long as he had to. And, if they never truly got together, he was still getting to spend time with the most beautiful woman he'd ever seen, even if it wasn't every day.

Though she carried herself with confidence, he'd also seen a vulnerable side of her. Somehow, she needed him to fill the role that he did. She craved his attention but had to keep him at arm's length for a reason that she wouldn't reveal. Maybe she'd been hurt badly by a man in the past. Maybe there was a family secret. There was no way to tell, and asking her would only get him the same answers he'd already gotten.

Andrea Ardelean was a study in contradiction. She spent her days helping her father keep the hotel running, and as far as he could tell, most of her nights alone. The shelves in her room, filled with hundreds of books, testified to the fact that she read extensively. He also knew that she spoke four languages, enjoyed art, and was one hell of a good cook.

Conversely, it also wasn't unusual to see her on scaffolding, painting, or repairing the plaster walls of the hotel. Once, he'd awakened in the middle of the night to find her hanging over the third-floor balcony, dusting the top of the chandelier that hung in the lobby.

She was a beautiful woman with a smile that could paralyze a man when she wanted it to. And, having seen her naked, he could testify to the exquisite form that she usually kept hidden beneath baggy tee shirts and jeans.

Truman moaned as he took a bite of the sandwich.

"Good?" she asked, one eyebrow arching slightly.

Truman nodded as he chewed. After washing the food down with a drink, he looked into her eyes. "The sandwich is almost as good as you look in that dress."

Andrea laughed. Picking up her drink, she nodded to an empty booth in the corner. "Care to join me?" she asked, not bothering to wait for an answer.

Truman picked up his drink and stood. As he followed her, he noticed that the eyes of every other man in the place was doing the same. A sense of accomplishment washed over him, knowing that every other man in the room was probably jealous. He wasn't the only one who recognized Andrea Ardelean as the most beautiful woman in town.

As Truman joined her at the table, she wrapped a hand around the small lamp on the table and blew out the flame. "Cozy," he said, sliding into the booth beside her.

"I don't like those things. All these open flames." She shook her head. "This old place is a tender box, you know."

"Mm-hmm." Truman watched his thumb wipe condensation from the glass. "So… I haven't seen you around much lately."

Andrea sipped her drink, surveying him over the rim of her glass. "I have many responsibilities that keep me busy. Have you missed me?"

"You are easy to look at, you know. When pretty things go missing, I tend to notice."

"I didn't ask if you noticed my absence. I asked if you missed me."

"I always miss you when you're not around," Truman said with a smile.

Andrea smiled. "Well, it is nice to be missed."

Truman watched her drink, envying the glass for being brought to her lips. There was a fluidity to the way she moved, unhurried, confident, that devoured his self-control. His hand reached out and brushed a lock of hair back, revealing the creamy skin of her slender neckline.

"You've been quite busy yourself," she said.

"Work's been a little hectic lately."

She shook her head, a coy smile coming to her lips. "I'm not talking about your work."

"What then?"

"Tell me," she began, putting her drink down. "How are things with you and this Tiffany Jasper?"

Truman retracted his hand and shrugged, his mood collapsing. "There's nothing to tell, really."

"That's not what I hear," Andrea said, a hint of tease in her voice.

Truman watched her stir her drink with a fingertip, then bring it to her mouth. "We went out on like three dates. Nothing big."

"Four," she corrected as one eyebrow inched upwards.

"Okay. Four dates. Like I said, not much to tell. There was nothing there, so I broke things off."

"Four dates…hmmm."

"What does that mean?" he asked.

"Don't people usually sleep together on the third date? Isn't that an unspoken rule?"

"I have no idea. I suppose some people do. Maybe some people do after the first date. I guess it depends on the people."

"Really?" she asked. "Do they?"

"That's what I hear."

"So, did you sleep with her?"

"That's kind of a personal question, don't you think?"

Andrea nodded, smiling at him. "I do think so. Yes."

"Well, for your information, the answer is no. I did not sleep with her."

She stared at him for a moment, gauging the truth in what he said. "Why not? Wasn't she attractive? Didn't you want to?"

"Well, she's pretty enough, I guess. And I am a guy, so I wouldn't have kicked her out of bed."

Andrea's smile flattened. "Hmm."

"I'm kidding." Truman nudged her with his shoulder. "It's a joke."

"You chose a bad time for your jokes."

"I know. It's a character flaw. I'm sorry." Truman put a hand on her arm as she thumbed condensation from her glass. "Anyway, I never really tried either."

"Hmm," she said again. She switched her drink to her free

hand and finished it.

"I didn't."

"Why not?" she asked, wiping the corner of her mouth with her fingertip.

Staring into her eyes, he wanted to say because she wasn't you, that every other woman in the world paled in comparison. He wanted to shout that he was in love with Andrea Ardelean and couldn't even think of another woman. He wanted to say all those things, but he didn't. He simply shrugged.

Andrea smiled, pushing her fingertips through the hair at his temple. "I believe you."

"Good."

"I must admit that I checked the registry to see if her name was in it."

Truman smiled, enjoying the hint of jealousy in Andrea's tone. "And she's not in it."

"She is not," Andrea replied with a smile. She looked down at her drink, then up at him. "Are you lonely, Truman? Is that why you went out with her?"

Truman sighed. "I went out with her because a friend of mine kinda set it up. She worries about me being alone. Why do you ask? We're not necessarily what you'd call an item, you know." Truman sipped his drink. "Are you jealous?"

She sighed. "Maybe I was. A little," she said, rolling the empty glass between her hands. She thought for a moment, then looked into his eyes. "Yes. I am."

Gazing into her eyes, Truman smiled. He'd come to the realization that he was in love with Andrea years ago and had even admitted to himself that he would marry her in an instant if she'd allow him. It felt good to know that she was jealous. It told him that this was more than a game to her.

"You have nothing to be jealous of."

"Don't I?" she asked, her eyes frantically searching his.

"No." In her eyes, Truman found a longing but also a sense of desperation and loneliness. "Believe me, Andrea, you have nothing to be jealous of."

"I have no right to be jealous."

"Maybe you do, maybe not. Either way, you don't need to be."

She smiled as her hand cupped his cheek. "Oh, Truman." A sigh escaped her as she looked at him. "Till the sun grows cold and the stars grow old."

"That's how long I'll—"

She put a finger on his lips. "Shhh. Please don't say it."

Truman puckered his lips and kissed her finger.

She slid her hand back to his cheek, her thumb caressing his skin. "Do you want to go upstairs and do things to me that will make us both ashamed to see my father in the morning?"

"There's nothing I'd love to do more. Do you want another drink?"

"No. There's a bottle of very old Scottish whiskey chilling in your room."

"What? I don't think so," Truman said, standing from the booth.

Andrea slid from the booth and straightened her dress. She ran a finger across his lips and down his chin. "I know there is because I put it there this afternoon." She offered a smile and a quick wink before turning and sauntering away.

The soft glow of the battery lamp next to the bed illuminated two entangled bodies as they staggered through the door of room 307. The heavy wooden door was barely closed behind them when Andrea grabbed Truman's tee shirt, shoving it over his head. She tore it from his raised arms and threw it aside as her mouth covered his neck with hungry kisses.

They moaned in unison as her hot mouth found his chest,

then his nipple. Her mouth opened wide, and her teeth were against his flesh. Truman grimaced as she bit down, holding him between her teeth.

"My god," she breathed as she released him. "I need you tonight."

Truman's hands found her butt, gripping it tightly as he pulled her into his erection. He moaned again as her mouth roved over his chest, delivering another bite that hovered somewhere between pain and pleasure.

Her hands came up, digging her fingernails into the flesh of his ribs as she pushed away from him. She flicked her head, tossing her tussled hair over one shoulder. Her fingertips left long scratches on his sides as they released him, coming up to find the zipper of her dress. In one smooth motion, she unzipped it and shimmied it down her body until it lay in a pool at her feet.

Truman groaned as she stood before him, completely naked. His eyes feasted on her lean, muscular body as the dim light danced along her masterpiece of creamy skin. Her full breasts rose and fell with each heavy breath, beckoning him.

The gentle curves of her hips swayed as she backed slowly toward the bed, calling him to her with one finger. "I didn't come here just to be looked at."

Truman crossed the room quickly, leaving his jeans on the floor. He fell on her, one hand finding her breast while the other sank into her hair. She arched her back to him in a moan as his fist closed around her hair.

He pressed his lips to hers. Their bodies moved into alignment. She gasped as he entered her, raising her hips to meet him. When he was fully within, her legs wrapped around his waist, holding him deep inside her.

Truman closed his eyes, relishing the moment. Sleeping with Andrea was so much more than he'd ever experienced before. It was more than sex. It was a coupling, a unification of souls, a giving of everything they had to pleasure the other and drawing pleasure from that giving.

When he opened his eyes, he looked into the green eyes peering up at him from a sea of auburn hair spilled across his pillow. Her eyes were wide and bright with excitement and hunger. Their sex was always frantic, but there was a desire in her eyes that told him tonight would be far beyond the usual.

He opened his mouth to speak, but she put a finger to his lips. "No words," she whispered. "Show me everything you want to say."

Truman lowered his body to hers as he moved in and out of her slowly. His lips found hers in a gentle kiss, then moved across her cheek and onto her neck. He sank his face into her hair, slipping his arms beneath her. Holding her to his chest, he brought his hips forward with a sudden thrust. When she gasped, he did it again.

Her legs fell to the bed, pushing back against him with each thrust. Her fingernails found his hips as their bodies came together, yanking him to her with each push.

Truman moaned as her body arched violently beneath him. A quiet whimper escaped her as she reached climax. Her arms and legs wrapped around him again, pulling him to her body and holding him tightly.

"I'm not done with you yet," she whispered into his ear.

"I certainly hope not."

CHAPTER TEN

June 4th. Kill Day. Mid Morning

An insistent buzzing pierced the darkness, dragging Truman from a deep, sated sleep. He grunted in protest as his hand reached from beneath the covers, probing the darkness. He found his bedside table and felt along it for whatever rude device was making the noise.

Finally, his hand landed on a cell phone, and he lifted it, casting the darkened room in an eerie glow. His thoughts went immediately to Andrea, and he turned in the bed. Her pillows were stacked neatly, and the covers had been put back in place on her side of the bed, but she was gone.

He sighed, climbing out of his slumber with each buzz of the phone in his hand. He answered it, then cleared his throat before pressing it to his ear.

"Hello."

"Well, hello there, sleepyhead."

Anthony Swails' gruff voice brought him fully awake. "Good morning, sir."

"I'm sure it is if you didn't spend the night on a cot with a hundred snoring assholes. We've been trying to reach you for a while now. I was getting ready to send someone by to check on you."

"Yes, sir. I'm sorry. I was up late last night." Truman thought for a moment, then added, "Watching things over here. At the hotel."

A chuckle came through the line, and then his boss asked, "Is that what they're calling it nowadays?"

"What? No. I mean—"

"Simmer down," Anthony told him with a laugh. "I'm just messing with you. I just wanted to check-in. I'm up at the school. These damned cots get worse every year. I should have brought an air mattress like you suggested."

"Are you going to survive?" Truman rubbed one eye with his fist.

"Oh, I'll be fine. The coffee sucks, and I swear to God, every single person here has a phone or tablet or some other device in front of their face."

"We're slaves to technology," Truman said, stifling a yawn.

"Things got a little exciting when everyone started looking for a plug, but we got it all sorted out eventually. Once everyone settled in, it was a calm night."

"Yeah, same here." Truman rubbed his face, forcing his mind to work. "Tommy Ledbetter is here this year. Guess he's staying in the hotel. He was drinking in the bar last night. Luckily, he stayed away from the hard stuff, but he did shut the place down."

"Yeah, Allen is here with me, but Brian is at City Hall. That's where Tommy usually goes. Brian said he wasn't there. I was wondering where he ended up."

"Lucky me, he's here."

"Well, he just has to stagger upstairs, so I guess there's no harm in him getting drunk. Y'all full up?"

"Full to the gills, according to Jean." Truman threw the covers back and sat up on the edge of the bed. "Chief, there's a family here from out of town. The guy said they were passing through and had car trouble. He was asking questions, so I filled him in on the cover story. I think he bought it. I did promise to get his hotel fees waived, so that'll come across your desk."

"I heard. Jimmy called me. Maybe that's not a bad thing, them being there. There's never been an attack on the hotel. Hopefully, it'll stay that way, and they can be on their merry way, none the wiser when all of this shit is over."

"Yeah," Truman agreed through another yawn. "Ben has some folks in his place across the street. I told him to make sure to keep stuff quiet and to sell them on the story."

"Out of towners?"

"Yup."

"Damn him."

"That's pretty much what I thought about it too. I told him you'd be pissed, but he said the mayor gave him the okay."

"That figures. What an asshole. Think he'll sell them on it?"

"You know, Ben. If he could make a dollar, he'd lie to his own mother. I think we'll be okay. He's a sleazeball, but he ain't stupid."

"True. Anything else?" Anthony asked.

"Nothing except for the Presbyterians having the church lit up like a Christmas tree."

"Yeah. I heard about that, too. There's nothing we can do about it. Stupid is stupid. Maybe the bad singing will keep any trouble away."

Truman rubbed his head and stretched his stiff back as the chief complained about the mayor. The night with Andrea had driven any thought of the date from his mind, and he didn't welcome the return of the subject. His head hurt, and his stomach was in knots from the scotch. His legs bore the usual burn that came from spending the night with Andrea, yet his spirits were high.

Last night was a blur of drinks and sex, of emotions and raw sexuality. When they both finally collapsed in the bed, sweaty and tired, he'd fallen asleep within seconds.

The scent of her perfume still clung to him, and his body longed to lie next to her. He wanted to search the hotel until he found her, whisk her into his arms, and bring her back to bed. He wanted to lay with her, their bodies coiled into one, and forget about what today was.

"You up for last-minute patrols today?"

"Yeah." Snatched from his thoughts of last night, the smile on his face faded quickly. "Of course," Truman lied. "Whatever you need."

"I'm staying here to watch over this crowd. I'm going to see if I can move to an office or classroom or something tonight. The missus wants some privacy, and the gym ain't cutting it. I think half of this town snores."

"Don't you usually do that anyway?"

"Yeah, but after our little talk with mayor dumbass, I thought I'd sleep in the gym."

Truman stifled a yawn. "Makes sense."

"Well, it sucks. Anyway, Allen and Brian will take the east and north ends of town. You take the west end. That is if you feel up to it."

Truman rolled his eyes as another chuckle came through his phone. News traveled fast in Friendly, especially when people were cooped up and bored. When this was over, there wouldn't be a secret left within twenty miles of town.

"Yes, sir. I'll get a bite to eat, then get right on it."

"Truman, be careful. Make sure you're back inside well before dark."

"I know. I will. You do the same."

The three-day sequester was an abundance of caution.

June third was safe enough, at least until midnight. The fourth, today, was "kill day." The fifth was clean-up day. The early day had been implemented to keep people from waiting till the last minute to prepare. Once, nine years ago, a family at the edge of town waited too long and was caught unprepared. The man, his wife, and their twelve-year-old daughter were all killed.

The day after was to avoid the lookie-loos and picture takers, sparing the families of those killed the inhumanity of the morbidly curious.

"Check in when you're back inside."

"Yes, sir. Be safe."

"You do the same. And remember, Truman, you're not a young man anymore."

The line went dead mid-chuckle as the Chief ended the call. Truman shook his head and dropped the phone on the bed beside him. Locking his fingers behind his head, he fell back onto his pillow with a smile. Having people know he was holed up with Andrea wasn't a terrible thing. Most of the men in town would give their eye teeth to be him. But doing it while people might be dying didn't have the best optics. It would put him right up there with Been Steely, and he didn't like that.

Still…

Truman closed his eyes, remembering last night. Andrea had maneuvered her body above him and sat up. Her hands swept her hair up on top of her head as her hips moved gently back and forth. His hands found the gentle curve of her hips, gripping her supple skin. A moan escaped her, and she released her hair, letting it fall about her shoulders. Her hands swept down her body and found his. Their fingers intertwined, then she bent forward, pinning his hands to the bed next to his head.

"I have you now," she whispered. Leaning close, her lips brushed against his as her hair fell around his face, closing off the world outside.

The light from the lamp next to the bed shone through her hair, turning it into a curtain of fire and her eyes into glowing green embers. He stared at her, consumed by the hungry look on her face.

Her eyes narrowed slightly, forming a tiny crease between them as she stared at him with a gaze that was borderline violent, as if energy pent up for a long time wanted to be free. He'd never seen her look at him that way. It was almost animalistic. Primal. But he loved it.

A knock on his door pulled him from his thoughts. He found the light by his bed and pressed the button on the side. Looking around in the dim glow, he found the pair of jeans he'd been wearing last night folding neatly in a chair. A smile came to his lips, knowing that it was Andrea who'd folded them. He pulled them on as he hobbled across the room. When he opened the door, he found Andrea's smiling face staring back at him.

"Good morning," he said with a smile of his own.

"Did I wake you?" she asked.

"No. But I was just thinking about you."

"Good." She put her palms on his chest and moved him into the room. Closing the door with her foot, her arms snaked around him as she pressed her body against his. Her lips met his in a passionate kiss. When she finally broke the kiss, she drug her fingertips lightly down his back, sending a shiver through his body. She stopped suddenly when her hand came to a series of welts.

Turning him to afford her a view of his back, she gasped. "Did I do that?" Her fingertips danced along the scratches, some of them caked with specks of dried blood. "I'm so sorry."

"Shh." Truman turned back to her. "Don't apologize for anything we did last night. It was beyond amazing."

Her hand went to a bruise surrounding his left nipple. She leaned in and kissed it. "I get carried away sometimes. I'm so sorry."

"Don't be," he said, smiling. "I didn't complain last night, and I'm not complaining now." He pulled her to him and kissed her lips.

Andrea laced her fingers together in the small of his back and laid her head on his bare chest. She sighed contentedly and nuzzled into him.

"I wondered where you went."

"I had to help Papa with breakfast and lunch. I have been awake for hours. People still must eat, and the hotel is full of people."

"I guess it is." He breathed in her scent, relinquishing it slowly. "Do you want to go back to bed?"

"I could lay with you in my arms and sleep a contented sleep for a hundred years."

"Mmm. That sounds wonderful."

"But you must do your police work. No?"

Truman groaned as his mood fell. "I do. Will you be here when I get back?"

"Where would I go? We're in the sequester, remember? Or did last night erase your memory?"

Truman smiled. "It did, of everything and everyone but you." His hands found her taunt backside, cupping each cheek through her jeans. He squeezed her to him with a quiet moan. "But I meant here, in my room. In my bed."

"Do you want me to be here when you get back?" she asked quietly, gently caressing his back.

"I very much do. Yes."

She looked up at him and smiled. "I'll be here for a while, then I have to help Papa prepare dinner and clean things up. If I'm not here, I'll find you later."

"Deal." Truman wrapped her in a tight embrace. Holding her in his arms, he sighed into her hair, wondering what the hell was wrong with him. In just a few hours, people would die, and all he could think about was being with Andrea.

Despite his self-admonition, when she nestled her body close to his, the thought of abandoning his patrol and taking her back to bed ran through his mind. There was just something about her that hooked him.

No, he admitted to himself. It wasn't something. It was everything about her that hooked him. Though attractive, Tiffany Jasper and every other woman he'd dated since his divorce paled in comparison to the aloof woman in his arms. Hell, in hindsight, even his wife never made him feel the way Andrea did. He could have remarried a few times since his divorce, but he always knew he couldn't stay away from Andrea. The very sight of her ignited a fire deep within him that only she could quench.

"You should go."

"I really should," Truman finally said, though without much conviction.

"Okay," she said through a yawn as she pulled away. "Mind if I take a nap here? I am hiding from Papa and everybody who might want something." She'd already slipped the jeans over her hips and let them drop to the floor when he agreed.

Truman groaned internally as he watched her move, the gentle curve of her bare butt peeking from beneath the bottom of her tee shirt. She crawled beneath the covers with a quiet moan of contentment and settled into his pillow.

"I really do have to go," he said again, this time with less conviction. Seeing her in his bed melted any sense of duty within him. Nothing else in his whole life had ever mattered as much as her. He shook his head. To hell with the patrol.

He started toward the bed. Why shouldn't he enjoy today? There was nothing he could do. Whatever happened would happen whether he went on patrol or not. Why not spend the day with the woman he loved?

Truman stopped halfway across the room when the gentle sound of sleep filled the air. Raising the lamp, he found Andrea nestled deep beneath his covers, curled in a ball on her left side. Her face was as peaceful and calm as a baby's. Her beautiful eyes were closed.

His chest swelled with emotion. "My god, I love you," he whispered. Forbidden by her from speaking them, the words felt good on his lips. He knew they were true, and somewhere deep inside, she knew it too. He was sure of it. There was no way she couldn't know.

Moving to the bedside, he swept the hair from her face and planted a kiss on her forehead. She stirred but didn't wake. He smiled as he watched her sleep. She barely resembled the woman he'd spent the night with. Last night, there were flames of hunger and passion in her eyes. Last night, her hands and her mouth had devoured him as if she hadn't seen him in years. Last night, she'd been insatiable.

Truman sighed, forcing himself to let her rest. He gathered some clean clothes and headed for the shower, hoping she'd sleep until he returned. Pausing in the bathroom doorway, he spared her another glance. Anything more, and he'd surely stay. The sooner he started his patrol, the sooner it would be finished, and he could be with her again. That was all that mattered now.

CHAPTER ELEVEN

June 4th. Kill Day. Early Afternoon.

Truman squinted at the brightness of the day as he stepped from the Jupiter Hotel. Standing on the sidewalk, he turned and looked back at the doors. They were beautiful and historic, but the best thing he could think about them just now was the fact that they led back to Andrea.

He rubbed his eyes with his fist and forced himself to turn away. He had a commitment to fill, a duty to do. He stumbled to his car, his mind battling every step. But what about his duty to himself? What about what he wanted?

And people want to live, but they won't, he admonished himself. He spared another glance at the doors, then turned away. Before him, the shadow of the sign atop the building lay along the deserted street. The gentle curves of the shadow reminded him of Andrea, and he turned back to the building. His eyes found the window to her room, and again, the desire to go to her rose in his chest. Though she wasn't in her room, it was hers. Her things were there. The sense of her was there and that was enough.

Shaking his head, Truman forced his eyes from the darkened window. Shielding his eyes, he scanned the deserted street. All of downtown was abandoned and eerily quiet. Heat rose from the pavement in waves, giving the old buildings an ominous look.

These last patrols were almost as bad as cleanup day. It always reminded him of the ghost towns he saw in movies, but he knew that wasn't the case. People weren't gone. They were hiding. Behind every boarded-up window was an agonizing family, waiting for the night and praying to be spared. Any one of them might not live to see the sun rise tomorrow.

He sighed and slipped a pair of sunglasses over his eyes as he opened the door to his cruiser. Though technically "kill day," it wasn't as dangerous as they led people to think. As far as they could tell, no one had ever been killed during the day, but a long night did lay ahead of them.

He started the car and switched on the radio. "Malone about to begin patrol of west side from Tuttle Street to the edge of jurisdiction."

"Roger," came a woman's voice over the radio. Maxine, the dispatcher, and her family always stayed at the police station in the center of town. "Be safe, Truman." Her normally cheerful voice was quieter, more somber.

"Roger that. Will do. You do the same. Truman out." He replaced the radio, then backed out of his space and headed west. As his eyes scanned the empty storefronts, the memories of last night's revelry faded. His thoughts wandered to the creature.

Nobody knew what it was because anyone who saw it didn't live to tell. Whatever it was, it was strong, had sharp claws, and liked blood. It was easy to see how most people were led straight to the possibility of a vampire, but he couldn't bring himself to believe it. In all that he'd read about vampires, they rarely tore their victims up so badly. There was a viciousness to these kills, a rage that he'd never seen before. And besides, he reminded himself, there's no such thing as vampires.

A part of him wanted to see the creature, to know exactly what it was. More than morbid curiosity, he wanted to erase the glimmers of doubt that danced through his mind. There was a part of him that rose to the surface sometimes that didn't believe there was a creature at all, despite seeing the evidence. His mind wanted to create a logical explanation for what happened every year. He wanted it to be a cult or some ritualistic killings. As bad as that was, it would make more sense.

He'd always equated living in Friendly to having a new shirt with a dark stain on it. If you covered the stain, everything looked fine, but you knew it was still there. Did it ruin the whole shirt? Should you throw it out? What if everybody agreed not to mention the stain? Would that be okay? Could you go on wearing it?

Sometimes, the surreal nature of life in Friendly amazed him, even after all these years. Any sane person would leave, yet most people didn't. So great was the gravitational pull of their small town life that they stayed, endured, buried the dead, and got on with their life. It was an annual game of Russian roulette played over and over and over.

Though he'd been through many sequesters, he didn't fully know what the people were going through. There had never been an attack at the hotel, the school, or the church. And even if there was an attack at the hotel, there were many windows. The chance of the creature breaking through his was small. Statistically, his chance of being attacked was negligible.

Of course, he couldn't judge anyone anyway. He'd done the same thing. He'd stayed, but he only had one reason, and it wasn't small town inertia. If Andrea wasn't here, he'd leave in a minute.

Lost in thought as he went through the motions of patrolling, Truman didn't see the kid until he'd crossed the sidewalk and was in the street. He'd come from the alleyway next to Josephine's Fabrics and was headed right for him, slumped over with his hand holding his stomach. The right side of his head and neck, his hands, and his stomach were drenched in red.

Truman slammed on the brakes and grabbed the radio, watching the kid's approach through the windshield. "Code Three, Main Street and Seventh Ave." He tossed the radio aside and sprung from the car. Rounding the hood, he watched the teenager stagger up to him. A thick red froth bubbled from the corners of his mouth. His loud moans echoed in the silence.

"What happened?" Truman asked, grabbing the kid as he fell against the hood of the car. Writhing in pain, the boy's hands left long red streaks on the white paint.

"Hang in there, kid. Shit. An ambulance is on the way. Fuck. What happened? Was it the creature?"

"Y-Yes. The creature," the boy croaked, rolling onto his back to look at Truman. His face was contorted with pain, his eyes begging for help.

"Shit," Truman exclaimed, his heart pounding against his chest as his eyes frantically scanned the area. "Where was it? Where'd this happen? Shit. Hang in there, kid."

"Over there." The kid waved a hand in the direction he'd come. "It came out of nowhere."

"Okay. You just hang in there, okay? Did you see it?"

"Big. Ugly." The boy's hand slid from his neck, revealing a large, swollen mass. Two black dots about an inch apart marked the bloody contusion. Puncture wounds.

"I-I'm a vampire now," the boy said, grimacing as he coughed more blood across the hood.

"Don't talk. Just hang in there. Holy shit."

The boy reached up and touched Truman's face with one cold hand, smearing sticky, red fingerprints on his skin. "I-I'm a vam…pire…and I need…I need you to call my mummy."

Truman stared in disbelief as the boy burst into a fit of laughter. He stood from the hood of the car, pointing at Truman. A second later, two more boys joined in from the alleyway behind them. "We so got you, dude."

"What the hell?" Truman looked between the two boys and the one before him. He was laughing hysterically and pointing one blood smeared hand at him.

"You stupid kids," Truman spat, realizing the prank. "What is wrong with y'all? That shit ain't funny."

"Chill, bruh." The boy next to him bent in laughter. "That was epic! Call my mummy. You should have seen your face. I really had you—hey!"

Truman moved quickly, spinning the kid around and slamming him back onto the hood face down. Before the kid had time to resist, handcuffs were on his wrists. Truman grabbed the boy by the collar of his tee shirt and drug him to the back of his car. Shoving him inside, he went after the other two. They turned and ran, disappearing before he made it to the alley.

"Stupid kids." He spat on the ground and wiped his face on the way back to his car. "Stupid shit," he added, looking at the stringy red substance on his fingers. He reached for the door handle as two other patrols pulled up, sirens wailing.

Truman waved his hands to calm the situation as the other two officers bailed out of their cars, guns drawn. "Sorry, guys. False alarm, but we do have some teenagers running around town trying to be funny." Truman looked in the back of his car. "I'm taking this dumbass to spend the night with Maxine. I'll call the chief on the way and explain. The other two ran down the alley by the fabric store. Hopefully headed home."

"Damned kids." Allen Banks was tall but thin and had an ornery disposition when riled up. He shoved his gun back into its holster and pulled out his nightstick as he started for the alley. "If I catch them little bastards…"

"Idiots. Where are their parents?" Brian asked as he followed Allen. "Jesus freaking Christ."

Truman got back into his car and looked over the seat at

his prisoner.

"Shit, bruh. That's like police brutality or something. I want, like, a lawyer or something."

"Shut up, dumbass. That was a very stupid thing to do. What's your name, kid?"

"Puddintaine," the kid shot back with a smirk.

Truman clenched his jaw and shook his head. "Okay, smart ass, you want to be that way about it. We'll see how a night in jail suits you. Then, after your parents get hold of you, I'm sure you'll be singing a different tune."

"Naw, man. You can't do that. It was just a joke."

"Not very funny now. Is it?"

"Not anymore. Look, bruh, just take me home. I'll stay inside. I promise. I'm sorry. It was just a dumb joke."

Truman grunted as he shoved a hand through his hair. "That's right. It was dumb. You don't get it, do you? The curfew is for your protection."

"My folks are gonna kill me, man," the kid protested.

"Better them than the creature." Truman shook his head. "Damn. You're an idiot. You just don't get it."

"What's to get? I mean, we're all just sitting around like a bunch of mental patients waiting to be sucked dry by this thing. Mom and Dad are bickering about every little thing. We've already played Parcheesi three times. Three times, man. I couldn't stand another minute of it. Everybody's all tense. It's crazy."

"The whole town is tense, kid."

"Why don't y'all just find it and kill it or something already? Damn, bruh."

"This ain't the movies, kid. That's not how stuff works." Truman turned his car around and headed to the jail. He wiped red goop from his cheek with the back of his hand and looked at it.

"What is this stuff?"

"Just some leftover blood from Halloween, I think."

Taking a deep breath, Truman let it out slowly, trying to calm himself.

"My dad said we just hide and wait. That's bullshit."

"You got a better idea?"

"Yes. I say we hunt it down and kill it."

"They tried that before you were born, kiddo."

"And?"

"And they found every one of them dead as a doornail."

"Holy shit. Really?"

"Really. And watch your mouth, kid. Do you talk that way in front of your mother?" Truman looked in his rearview mirror at his charge. The boy was near tears in anticipation of what his parents would do. "Look, I'm sorry if I got a little rough with you. Everyone is pretty tense right now."

"Dude," the boy said, shaking his head. "This is bullsh— messed up. When I'm old enough, I'm leaving this psycho assed town."

"That's probably the smartest thing you've said all day, and again, watch your mouth."

The kid replied with a huff. "Why don't you just leave? Why doesn't everybody?"

Truman spared the kid another glance in the mirror. "It's complicated," he said, for lack of a better answer. "I mean, people can't just move. Folks around here aren't sitting on a pile of money, you know. Moving is expensive. You'd have to sell your house, then what would that accomplish? It'd be the same thing, just with different people."

"Still," the kid persisted. "Save up or something." He shook his head. "What about you? Why don't you leave then? Cops make good money, don't y'all?"

The thought of Andrea was the first to cross Truman's mind, but he refused to admit it to the kid. "I'm a cop. People here need more help than anybody else, I reckon."

"Whatever, man. I'm out of here the first chance I get. I turn eighteen in a year and a half, and you'll never see me again."

"Well," Truman said as he rolled to a stop in front of the square brick building that served as the police station. "Maybe you'll learn your lesson and get that chance someday. But tonight, you're spending time in a cell. C'mon kid. Maxine is going to love you."

Truman stopped his car on the brick-paved streets of what people referred to as "old town." The term always amused him because the rest of the town wasn't much newer. He parked alongside the curb, occupying three empty spots angled to the sidewalk. It wasn't like anyone else would need them.

Getting out, he was greeted by the heat of the day. On top of last night's activities, the rush of adrenaline from the kid's prank had drained his energy. He groaned and shut the door.

The last part of his patrol was a walkthrough of the downtown shops. Having no one in them, they weren't in danger of attack, but the owners did worry about the possibility of looting. It had never happened, but the Chief promised one final walkthrough to quell their fears and assure that they'd stay home.

Walking to the shade beneath the awning in front of Clair's Jewelry Store, Truman sighed heavily. He wanted to go back home and find Andrea, but the kid he'd hauled in earlier had sparked a line of thought, and his patrol had afforded him some time to think.

He knew that the reason he'd given the kid for staying in Friendly was a lie. Maybe the kid did, too. His and Andrea's romance didn't seem to be as secret as he'd thought.

The thing that kept his mind busy was the idea of what he was willing to risk just to be with her on the occasions she chose to be with him. He could escape the specter of the creature, but he could never escape his feelings for her. The fact that he'd risk his own life for the chance to be with her was a profound one that had never occurred to him before. He'd known for a long time that he loved her but had never quantified it like that before.

Motorboating his lips as he exhaled, Truman looked at his reflection in the glass storefront. He was just under six feet tall and had put on a few pounds in the last ten years. He had a "dad bod" despite having no children, and his hair wasn't as thick and full as it once was. There were lines on his face that didn't use to be there. All in all, he considered himself average for a man his age, leading to the question of what Andrea saw in him.

She was exquisite in both mind and body. There was an old school charm to her like no one else he'd ever met. In many ways, she was like a princess, but at the same time, she drank and knew how to have fun. She served her father dutifully yet still hid the fact that they were lovers from him. If not, Jean was good at pretending she did.

"Stop it," he told himself aloud. "Stop thinking so damned much and just enjoy it." He ran a hand over his hair and closed his eyes, wishing he could do just that. Just stop thinking about it and enjoy it for what it was.

When he opened his eyes, they shifted the focus from his reflection to the store beyond the glass. A case just inside the window displayed several pendant necklaces. His eyes drifted to an emerald roughly the size of his thumbnail, surrounded by diamonds. The thought that it would look beautiful on Andrea swam into his mind. Immediately afterward, he wondered what it cost and cringed.

"No," he told himself. He decided to buy it for her and wasn't going to let his cheap side talk him out of it. Of course, he'd rather buy a wedding ring, but he knew she wouldn't accept it. Would she accept such an expensive gift from him?

She wore jewelry occasionally, so why wouldn't she? Green would look good with her red hair. It wasn't gaudy, but it wasn't small either. The more he looked at it, the more perfect it became.

Finally, nodding, he made up his mind. As soon as this was over, he was coming straight down here to get it. He'd go to her room and give it to her. If she tried to refuse, he'd insist she take it. She'd wear it and think of him, and she'd be happy. He'd see her wearing it, and he'd be happy. Everyone would be happy.

Everyone except the people who die tonight. And their families.

Truman let his head fall back with a groan as the notion smashed his thoughts of Andrea. "God, I hate being a cop in this town."

Turning from the store window, his mind began toying with the idea of what he'd be if he wasn't a policeman. He wouldn't have to board up old ladies' windows, work nights, or clean up dead bodies. He wouldn't have to worry about the creature anymore. The kid's statement that cops made "good" money was a bit of an overstatement. He could find plenty of jobs that paid as well. Even at fifty. Even in a small town.

If he weren't a cop, he could have stayed with Andrea today instead of sweating it out on a stupid patrol of an empty town. He could have pulled her to him, their bodies so close that he could feel her heart beating. The smell of her would envelop the bed. Everything outside of his bedroom wouldn't exist. There'd be no smart-assed kids. No deserted town. No creature. He wouldn't see the boarded-up houses or think about what was happening. He could pretend none of this was real and snuggle closer to her.

The image of her in his bed surfaced in his mind, and he smiled as a realization came to mind. That's what had been bothering him these last few weeks. He was just tired of it all. He was tired of being a cop. Yeah, he thought, nodding. This is it.

I'm done.

He fished the cell phone from his pocket and dialed a familiar number. When a gruff voice answered. He said, "Hey, Anthony, we need to talk."

CHAPTER TWELVE

June 4th. Kill Day. Afternoon.

Truman stood in the lobby of the Jupiter Hotel and turned his phone off. Behind him, the same men who'd let him out earlier were back at work, replacing the sheets of plywood over the door.

The randomness of the attacks left people unsure of what drew the creature. Speculating that it might be either the sound of a phone ringing or the radio waves it emitted, most people turned theirs off completely. No one was willing to find out the hard way.

The police force usually kept theirs on silent, set to vibrate. They wouldn't respond to a call, but if one came in, Maxine would relay it via a group text message to them. That way, they'd all know where to meet in the morning.

Truman would no longer be getting those texts. For so many years, he'd tracked the messages, spending agonizing hours watching his phone for the alerts. Through the dispatcher, he'd get updates on where and when the attacks happened in as close to real-time as he cared to be.

He would no longer have to worry about that, but the apprehension remained. People would still die. Messages would still go out. The other officers, men he considered friends, would get them. The only thing that had changed about the night was his participation in it.

He wasn't going out in the morning or any other morning. He'd had a long conversation with Anthony Swails, confiding in him his hopes and wishes. In the end, his boss accepted his resignation willingly enough, even thanking him for his years of loyal service. They'd even talked about his eligibility for retirement and a city pension, which calmed some of Truman's concerns about his finances. He was planning to make a big purchase and was worried about his savings taking such a hit.

In the end, things went better than he'd hoped. The chief had even joked about what Truman would do to fill his time now that he didn't have to work the occasional night shift.

Looking up, he watched the hotel staff as they reinforced the doors. The four feet by eight feet sheets of plywood had been painted purple and green to match the Jupiter's aesthetic but also to calm the guests. Seeing the plain plywood only served to remind everyone what was happening outside. This way, it was easier to pretend that their friends and neighbors weren't being exsanguinated.

Turning away from the workers with a sigh, Truman determined to change his thoughts from the day to what he hoped would happen tonight. The best way to do this was to find Andrea, so he headed for the dining room.

The patrons, not hiding in their rooms or drinking in the bar, had gathered in clusters at some of the larger tables. A few of them spared him a collective glance as he entered the room. A pall hung on their faces despite their attempts at a polite smile. In their eyes was a shared knowledge of what tonight was. One man nodded to him. No one spoke.

Three couples were at the first table he passed, in the middle of what looked like an evenly matched game of Monopoly. Thomas Spencer, a large man who ran the Swipe and Swap held a colorful array of money in one of his meaty fists like he was throwing dice in a back alley. His wife was moving a metal slice of pizza around the board. She landed on St. James Place, and someone celebrated quietly while she moaned in frustration.

Another group had a game of spades going. Beyond them, a few old men were in the process of shuffling dominoes. The porcelain pieces rattled noisily in the quiet despite their best efforts to be quiet.

The out-of-towners were huddled to themselves, playing the game of Life. The girl spun the wheel and then moved a green car around the board. Truman noticed that she didn't have a blue peg denoting a husband, but she did have three "pet" pegs.

Everyone else in the room was simply engaging in quiet conversation while they ate their sandwiches and chips around a flickering lamp. In the pale light, they looked like they were having a sad séance.

Truman made his way to the long tables set up at the far end of the dining room, near the kitchen. The neatly wrapped sandwiches were stacked in sections, each one marked with a hand-printed sign. He recognized the perfect, flowing script as Andrea's, and a smile slipped across his face. Tonight's menu included fried bologna, ham and cheese, and pimento cheese. Something for everybody.

He approached a middle-aged black woman tending the iced tea dispenser. Struggling to remember her name, he simply addressed her as "ma'am" and asked for Andrea. When she said she didn't know where Andrea was, he asked for Jean. The woman said that he wasn't feeling well and went to lie down a few hours ago.

Truman thanked her, trying hard to mask his disappointment as his spirit fell. If Jean didn't feel well, it would explain Andrea's absence. It also cast his plans for the night in doubt. Truman grabbed a fried bologna sandwich on his way out and headed for the steps. He didn't feel like drinking or playing games with anyone but Andrea. He'd been in his own head too much since finding the kid and just wanted to forget about everything happening.

Trudging up the stairs took some of the steam from Truman's disappointment but didn't resolve it completely. As he made the third-floor landing, he started toward his room but stopped and turned toward the other end of the hall. Andrea's room. The entire end of the hallway was dark, with no sliver of light slipping from beneath either hers or Jean's doors.

For a moment, he considered going to her room and knocking. He wanted to share his big news with her, to find out what she thought. He envisioned them discussing his options and his plans for the future. Maybe the change would be the catalyst she needed to solidify their relationship.

Standing alone in the dark hallway, he sighed, deciding not to intrude. He could wait. If her father didn't feel well, Andrea would be busy with the guests or tending to him. As badly as he wanted to see her, he refused to be a nuisance.

Turning, he started down the hall toward his room but stopped suddenly when he heard the faint sound of a door closing. He turned and looked back down the hall, but it was empty. The only other door on the floor was the roof access near his room. He hurried along the dark corridor and opened the door.

Pausing, he listened, but there was only silence. Finally, the policeman in him took over, and he pulled a penlight from his pocket. The faint light showed an empty hallway leading to a narrow staircase. No one else knew he'd quit the force, and the roof access needed to be barred. Especially tonight. He could stand being a cop for a bit longer.

At the top of the steps, he found a thick wooden plank standing against the wall. When placed in the brackets on the metal door, the slat would reinforce it, preventing it from opening.

His brow furrowed. Only Andrea, Jean, and himself lived on the third floor. Besides, it was getting late. No one should be outside.

Pushing the door open, he poked his head outside and looked around. The sun was low in the western sky, just ducking behind a forest of pine trees on a distant hill.

He shut the light off and stepped onto the roof, closing the door behind him. Rounding the small structure that housed the roof access, he saw Andrea standing at the far back corner of the roof, leaning on the parapet wall that surrounded the building. His heart rate climbed quickly, and a smile slipped across his lips. He'd get to see her after all.

As he watched, a gust of wind tore at her hair, blowing it into her face. One hand came up and pushed it back into place. When the wind blew her hair again, she let it stay. Crossing her arms, she released a long sigh and looked at the sky to the west.

There was a weight about her, a heaviness that looked foreign. Both hands came up and pushed through her hair. Gathering it at the nape of her neck, she swept it gently over her right shoulder.

Taking a step closer to the short wall that crowned the building, she put her hands on it and leaned over the side, peering down the wall. His brow furrowed as he watched, his heart aching for her. Something was bothering her, but what? Was she battling herself over their relationship as he'd done many times? If so, being the one to make the decision didn't look any easier than being the one to accept it.

"Don't jump," he finally said with a grin, slipping the light back into his pocket.

Andrea startled, turning to him with a hand on her chest. "Truman?"

"The one and only," he said with a smile as he crossed the roof. "Is everything okay? You seem upset."

She nodded, her smile widening. "Trapped between the

precipice and the stranger, the maiden had but two choices; give herself to him willingly or leap to her certain death."

"Wow. You sure know how to make a man feel good about himself."

"It is a very old play," she said, casting her eyes to the streaks of red hovering above the trees to the west of town. "Full of adventure, sex, and a forbidden love."

"Sounds interesting."

"Hmm." Andrea drug the hair from her face as she looked at him. "It is a play about hard choices that people must make."

"I know a little something about that." Truman looked at her, the news of his choice hanging on the tip of his tongue.

Andrea smiled, nodding gently. "Choices can be difficult."

"What did she do?"

"Hmm?"

"In the play?" he asked, nudging her gently with his shoulder. "What did the beautiful maiden do?"

"Well, the play was a tragedy so..." She trailed off, laughing softly.

"Well, in that case," Truman wrapped his arms around Andrea, embracing her from behind. "I'm going to hold on to you. You know, just to prevent any accidents."

"Please do," she said, settling her back into his chest. Her eyes went again to the clouds as she sighed. "It's quite beautiful, don't you think?"

"I do," he said, looking at Andrea. "The most beautiful thing I've ever seen."

She smiled and shook her head playfully. "I meant the sky."

"Me too," he said. "I can see it reflecting in your eyes."

She smiled at him, giving him a quick kiss before turning back to the dissolving sun. "Why must things be the way they are?"

"I don't know. Life usually has a way of punching you in the gut if you hang around long enough."

Andrea drew in a deep breath and released it slowly. "Were you hurt badly when your wife divorced you?"

Truman's brow furrowed, thrown by the question. "Uh. I suppose. I mean, it wasn't a complete surprise. Things weren't bad, but they weren't great either, you know." He nodded. "But yeah, I guess I was hurt by the finality of it all."

"Things weren't good. Why?"

Truman sighed. "You know, people get caught up in things. Time passes, and people change, I suppose, grow apart."

"And you've been alone since, haven't you?"

"More or less," he answered with a shrug.

"Why haven't you taken a new wife?"

Truman drew in a long breath and sighed. "Do you want to know the truth?"

"I do."

"At first, I was just angry, I guess. My life got turned upside down. Everything I'd worked for was gone. I had to start over, more or less. I suppose I was jealous, too. She remarried less than a year later."

"And now?" she asked.

"Now?" he asked.

"Why don't you take a wife now?"

"Because the only wife I want doesn't want to marry me."

Andrea twisted in his arms and slid her arms around his waist. She buried her face in his chest. "I'm sorry."

Truman stroked her hair, sensing her pain. "Oh," he said. "You thought I meant you? Wow. Uh. This is awkward."

Andrea poked him in the ribs. "You and your stupid jokes."

"I'm sorry. I can't help it."

"You know, it is just the way you avoid unpleasant things."

"I know. I'm sorry," he said, lifting her chin to look into her eyes. "Look, you said your life was complicated. I've known where you stand from the beginning. I appreciate your honesty."

"Yet you still want to be with me. Why?"

Truman shrugged. "I don't know. I just do. There's something about you that draws me. I can't explain it. Being with you is like a piece of me that's been missing has been put back into place. The truth is that there could never be anyone else."

Andrea squeezed him. "You deserve a good wife who will take care of you and give you a house full of children."

"Hold on now. I didn't say anything about kids," he said with a laugh. "Especially not a house full. What is that five? Ten? Good lord. I'd go crazy."

She slapped him playfully on the chest. "You know what I mean. You should marry a girl in town. Perhaps that blonde girl. Tiffany. I'm sure she would be a good wife for you." Andrea shook her head. "How long have you wasted with me? How many years have I stolen from you?"

"Not a single one. I have what I want," he said. "A small portion of gold is better than twice as much silver. I have enough."

"Then you are a fool, but I am lucky for it." Andrea sighed against his chest. After a long silence, she whispered, "Papa is unwell."

"I know. I asked after you in the kitchen, and they told me. Anything serious?"

"No. He is just old and very tired. He just needs to rest."

Truman nodded as he held her, looking over her shoulder as the sun slipped further behind the trees. It would be gone within minutes.

"As nice as this is, we should probably get back inside," he whispered. "It's almost nightfall."

"I know," she sighed. "I have much to do."

Andrea tried to pull away, but Truman held her. "Can I

see you tonight?" He felt her body tense against his, then added, "If you're busy, I understand."

"It's not that I don't want to."

"I know." His grip on her loosened just enough to lift her chin. He stared into her eyes and knew he'd made the right decision today. There was a wetness in them that spoke volumes to him. Her eyes said that she wanted to be with him, that she hungered to be in his arms.

"What?" she asked, matching his gaze.

In his mind, he told her of his love for her, about his plans, about how he wanted to be with her until the day he died. His lips parted, and he simply said, "Nothing."

"Nothing?" she asked.

"I was just thinking about how beautiful you are." His free hand swept a lock of hair back from her face. "And how I wish I could be with you forever."

"Forever is a very long time, Truman." She smiled and squeezed him, releasing a contented moan. "I wish I could stay here with you, but I do have things that will keep me from your arms, if only for a while."

"I know," he said, relinquishing his grip on her. "We need to get inside anyway. I'll make sure things are buttoned up here. You go ahead."

Truman watched her cross the roof. When she stopped at the door and looked back at him, he went to her. "Come to my room when you're done. Wake me if you have to."

Andrea smiled and kissed him before opening the door and disappearing into the darkened staircase.

"Do you need a light?" he asked, catching the door before it closed. Peering into the darkness, he listened for the sound of her footsteps. He pulled the penlight from his pocket and shined it into the stairway, but Andrea was already gone.

CHAPTER THIRTEEN

June 4th. Kill Day. Dusk.

Truman dropped his phone to the table next to the chair in his room and sighed loudly as he stretched. In the last few hours, he'd gone through most of his "sequester snacks," two beers, and scrolled through more social media than he'd seen in the last few months combined, but none of it could hold his attention.

Afforded an opportunity to relax, thoughts began to creep into his idle mind. He'd also heard the rumors about either the chief or mayor being the creature. He'd simply shrugged them off as nonsense. He would bet good money on not guilty, but he wouldn't go all in on either. He'd known both men for years and had found the chief nothing less than magnanimous. He didn't serve as chief for his own glory or power. He did it mostly because it was a hard job that no one else wanted.

Still, his mind persisted. It would be the perfect cover. He ran his hands briskly over his face several times. It wasn't the chief. This thing had plagued the town since way before he was born. It couldn't be him or the mayor either.

Dismissing the idea, his thoughts turned to Andrea, and a flat smile came to his lips. It was wonderful to have someone to desire so much, but that just made it harder when she was away from him. She was complicated, much of her life a mystery, but he didn't care. He'd come to realize that the time he spent with her was the only time he was truly happy anymore. The years in this town had worn on him, and she was his one reprieve.

There was an urgency in his need for her tonight, and that was something more than the date. He'd weathered plenty of June fourths alone and had never felt this way. He always wanted her, but tonight, it was more of a need, a deep ache. But not only for himself. It was as if she needed him too somehow, though he had no idea why.

There was something off about her that worried him. On the roof, he'd seen the longing in her eyes, but there was also a restlessness, a conflict that he didn't like. Did she sense that he wanted to take their relationship up a notch? Could she possibly know how he was feeling? Women were more intuitive than men, but he hadn't said anything to make her think that he did.

But what if she did? Did her restlessness mean that she didn't want him the same way he wanted her? Maybe there was someone else. Someone who didn't have to dip into their savings to buy a pendant for her. Perhaps someone younger, more handsome.

Shaking his head, he pushed the thought out of his mind. It wasn't another man. He'd have heard about it. But what was it? Was Jean badly sick? Maybe he had cancer. They were very private people. If he did, they wouldn't tell anyone. He seemed fine just yesterday.

And what was all that talk on the roof, asking how he handled things when his wife left him? Was she testing the waters in preparation for her own imminent departure? Was she feeling guilty, knowing she'd break his heart? Was she planning to leave? Where would she go? Why would she leave?

Maybe Jean was really sick and near death? Did Andrea just stay in this town as a duty to her father? To help run the hotel? Was that the only reason she stayed?

Truman stood with a grunt. He looked around his room, lit only by the small battery lamp next to his chair. His hopes for the evening were fading by the minute, and the room was beginning to feel small and cramped. Sleep was out of the question. All he'd do was think about Andrea and torture himself with a million unanswerable questions.

He walked into the bathroom and washed his face with cold water. Exiting the bathroom, he stood with his hands on his hips and surveyed the empty room before him. It suddenly felt small and lonely, depressing. Shaking his head with a sigh, he went to the door, hoping he'd find someone or something downstairs to distract him.

He made the landing and was about to turn and head to the first-floor, but familiar voices caught his attention. Turning, he ducked through the opening and into the hallway that wrapped around the cavernous stairway and served the guests on the second-floor.

The first door he came to was open, which wasn't unusual. Many people left their doors open in the early evening to invite company. Friendly was a close-knit community, and people liked to interact. To him, it was just another way of pretending that today wasn't today. The open door was a de facto front porch where people sat and waved at passing neighbors.

Peeping into the room, he saw Jerry and Elizabeth Smithson sitting on the bed. In their late forties, they were a couple friends of his and Megan, his former wife. The fact that he'd "gotten them in the divorce" was a running joke between them.

"Y'all not about to come to blows, are you?" he asked, glad to have some familiar company.

Both greeted him happily, and Jerry invited him in. Truman walked into the room and shook his head. A large, white sheet of canvas lay on the bed between them, on which a map of the town had been drawn. Dozens of red X's were scattered around the drawing.

"Oh, God. Not this old thing again," Truman said with a groan. Ebby, as everyone called her, and Jerry had been keeping up with the victims of the creature for as long as he could remember. They'd started it determined to flesh out a pattern but were no closer to figuring it out than ever.

"I'm telling you, this year it will be in quadrant four," Jerry said, pointing to the upper east side of town. He looked up at Truman and nodded confidently.

"You're nuts. Can you even see? It's gotta be the western end of town, somewhere around Fifth Avenue and Applewood or The Patterson Farm Road," Ebby replied, stabbing her finger to the canvas.

"Don't you think all this is a little morbid? I mean, Ebby, doesn't your folks live out there close to the Farm Road?"

"They do. That's why they're across the way in one of the suites."

"Smart girl." Truman shook his head. "Are either of you ever even remotely close?"

"Not yet," Jerry said, holding up a finger, "But I've got it figured out this year."

"You better hope he's wrong. You know who lives in that part of town?" Ebby asked with a coy smile. When Jerry gave her a queer look, she explained. "Tiffany Jasper lives in those apartments on Twelfth Street." She tapped her fingertip into the map.

The couple burst into laughter.

"Wow, it's just like grade school all over again. I'm outta here." Truman turned to leave, but they stopped him.

"Wait. Please. Check this out," Jerry called. "We're also trying to figure out *who* it is."

Truman turned back to them. "Don't you mean what it is?"

"Nope," Ebby said, shaking her head. She raised her eyebrows. "We think it's a who. Not a what."

Truman rolled his eyes. "Why not? That seems to be the trend lately." Truman grabbed a chair from the desk and pulled it to the bed. He sat in it backward and crossed his arms on the backrest. "I'm all ears. Do tell."

"Something wrong?" Jerry asked.

Truman waved him off. "Nah. Just a long day, is all. Go ahead."

"Well, obviously, it's a vampire," Ebby began.

"I mean, yeah, that's obvious," Jerry agreed, nodding.

"Is it now?" Truman asked. "You two sound pretty sure of yourselves."

"Yes," Ebby continued. "It has to be. Don't you see? I mean, maybe not a typical vampire, but it's a bloodsucker. No doubt."

"Okay. Say it is. What does that do for y'all's little fantasy," Truman said with a chuckle, waving his hand over the canvas.

"Scoff, if you will, but it has to be. Nothing else fits."

"And that means it's somebody in town," Ebby added, chiming in on the heels of Jerry's comment.

Truman held his hands up. "Hold up. That's dangerous talk. You'll end up turning everyone in town against people. It's a slippery slope, guys. Hell, we could end up with something like the Salem Witch Trials right here in Friendly. Are you forgetting there are only five of us cops? If things got out of hand, we'd be outgunned very fast."

Ebby threw a dismissive wave at him. "That part we're just keeping between us."

"Well, that's good," Truman said. "I'd hate to see people running around turning folks in for being a vampire because they like their steak cooked rare." Truman laughed. "But—" he held up a finger, "Out of curiosity, just who do y'all think it is?"

"Well," Ebby said, her eyes wide with excitement. "We've narrowed it down some but haven't zeroed in on any one person yet."

"Do me a favor. When you do, let us cops know first. Okay?"

"Oh, definitely," Jerry said. "We're no vampire slayers, dude."

"That's good to know. I wouldn't want to get a call about some little old guy with a wooden stake through his chest." Truman chuckled, rolling his eyes again. "Wow. You two crack me up."

"We're serious. Just think about it. It just affects the town and outlying areas. It stays close. This must be its base."

"Maybe it commutes to work," Truman said with a grin. Greyhound runs right through here every Thursday morning. Hell, there's a handful of strangers in town as we speak."

Ebby shook her head. "No. It lives here."

"Dipping your pen in the company ink is never smart." Truman laughed at his own joke, but the others didn't.

"Anyway," Jerry added, "It's common knowledge that vampires look like normal people when they're not hunting."

"Is it now? Common knowledge, I mean. I did not know that. How about that? Learn something new every day."

"Stop," Ebby said, shaking her head. "Seriously. We've really been looking into this."

"Let me guess, you went online?" Truman asked.

"Yes," Jerry added. "And in some pretty old books and stuff. I'm telling you. We'll figure it out. You wait and see. There's all kinda stuff out there, Truman. Now, obviously, a lot of it is plain crap, but there are some reliable sources if you know where to look."

Truman sighed. "Do me a favor. Just don't bring a bunch of folks into town to investigate this mess, okay? That's the last thing we need."

"Surely you agree that something must be done. I mean, we can't just keep on like this year after year."

"Hoping against hope that it's not our turn," Jerry added, reaching across the canvas to take Ebby's hand. "I mean, that's why we haven't had kids, Truman. We can't just sit back and let this keep happening."

"Look." Truman ran his hands through his hair and tilted his head back, staring at the ceiling. "I know that this sucks. Trust me. I've done too many cleanups. But this thing is dangerous, and sheltering really does limit the number of fatalities. This thing has been around for years. People have tried to kill it, and they ended up dead. I'm afraid I have to side with the Chief on this one, folks."

Truman rubbed his forehead and pushed a hand across his mouth. "We just met with the mayor today, and he basically said the same thing as y'all. When we asked him what we could do—" He held up his finger to silence Jerry before he could speak. "A feasible plan that makes sense and won't get a bunch of folks killed." He looked back and forth between his friends. "He didn't have one."

"But if we can find out who it is, we can approach them when they're normal," Jerry explained.

"Then what?" Truman asked with an incredulous grin.

"Then you arrest them."

"Just like that?" Truman snapped his fingers. "You don't think they'll just turn into whatever it turns into and kill us all? Do you think they'll just be like, 'Oh, well, you got me'? This isn't an episode of Scooby Doo, guys."

"We know that," Jerry said, stung by Truman's comment.

"That's the beauty of our plan. Once we narrow it down to three or four, we can contain them somehow this time next year and observe them."

"In the 'somehow' lies the problem, folks."

"But still, if it doesn't happen, we'll know we've got our man," Ebby said.

"Or woman," Jerry put in.

Truman pushed up from the chair with a sigh. "Jesus, you two. Just keep all this under wraps, please. Especially about the meeting with the mayor."

"Of course, man," Jerry said as Truman returned the chair next to the desk and started for the door.

"But don't you want to know who we suspect?" Ebby asked.

Truman stopped just short of the door and turned around. "I don't know. Something tells me that I probably don't." He tossed his hands into the air and let them fall. "Do I want to know?"

"I think you might," Ebby said with a flat grin.

"What's that supposed to mean?" Truman asked, coming back to the bed. "Who are you talking about?"

"This is just a preliminary list. Don't get upset," Jerry said, holding a hand up to calm Truman. "Nothing's sure yet."

Truman looked from Ebby to Jerry and back to Ebby. Sitting crossed-legged on the bed, she looked up at him as she chewed a thumbnail. "Why would I get upset? Am I on the list?"

"No," Ebby said with a laugh. She looked at her husband, then back to Truman. "But the chief is."

Truman laughed. "You two are nuts. You know that, right?"

"Now, wait a minute. Just think about it. What better way to isolate us and keep yourself from being seen? It's perfect. And you said yourself that the chief favors the sequester."

"Yeah, sure. Does the fact that the chief is always up at the school with a few hundred people figure into your equation?"

"Maybe he says he doesn't feel well and wants to go to

bed early," Jerry suggested. "That would make the perfect alibi. He's old. Old people go to bed early. Nobody would think twice about it."

Truman's mind went instantly to his conversation with this boss. He'd mentioned that he was going back to sleeping in a classroom for "privacy."

"Nope." Truman shook his head. "It's not the chief. That's absolutely ridiculous. Who else you got?"

"Maria Shaffer," Jerry said, looking at the paper in his hand.

"She's close to a hundred years old!" Truman shook his head with a laugh. "Damn."

"Vampires can live thousands of years. Plus, she's from Romania or someplace over there."

"She's from Friendly, Alabama, genius. She was born here," Truman said.

"You don't know that for certain. Records can be faked. Besides, her people are from that part of the world, and that's where vampires originated."

"I hate to break it to you, but vampires originated in Hollywood, my friends. They don't exist."

"Truman, I know you're a born skeptic, but if you read up on it, there's lots of proof. You just have to open your mind to it. Have you ever heard of Vlad the Impaler?"

"Guys, we're talking about dark ages and superstition and folklore. People were ignorant back then. They believed this stuff. We should know better by now."

"Then what is that thing if it's not a vampire?" Jerry asked.

Truman shrugged. "I don't know, but it's not a vampire."

"How do you know?"

Truman showed them his palms. "I said, don't know what it is." He shoved a hand through his hair. "I just…"

"Just what?" Ebby asked.

"Nothing. I just want this to be over. I'm tired of thinking about all this." Truman turned to leave but stopped again. "Please, just keep this to yourselves."

Nodding, Jerry assured him that they would, then looked at his wife. "Should we tell him?"

Truman stopped just short of the open door and turned around. "Tell me what?"

"Um," Ebby shared a nervous look with her husband. "Another name on the list is Jean Ardelean. He's from that part of the world, too."

"Transylvania," Jerry added.

"Stop." Truman held his hand up. "Stop right there. You two are just going to cause some innocent people a lot of grief. Jean is the nicest person I know. No. Take him off the list. Besides, he's only been in town for about ten years or so. It's not him."

"It's just that—" Ebby began.

"No. Just no. Jesus Christ." Truman shook his head. "This shit has been happening for a hundred years, probably. Nobody in town who is alive today could be involved. No. It's dangerous talk all the way around."

Truman walked to the door as thoughts of Jean Ardelean came to mind. Just like with the chief, he too would be out of the public eye tonight. Anger rose in his chest. He trusted both men completely, and both had just been named as suspects in the killings.

Ebby got up and followed him to the door. "Just stay a minute and listen." When Truman shook his head, she added, "Please."

Truman let her take the door from him and close it. "What else is there?"

"Look," Ebby began as she went back to the bed. "There are things we can't fully explain. That doesn't mean they're not real."

"Yeah," Jerry put in. "The whole thing about truth being stranger than fiction, you know."

"Maybe in some cases, but all this," Truman waved his hand at the map. "This is just nuts."

"I agree," Jerry said. "The fact that something kills people in this town every June fourth is nuts. What's even more nuts is that everyone doesn't just move the hell away."

"We've talked about it, but we never actually ever do move. Maybe because nobody close to us has been taken." Ebby shrugged. "None of this makes any sense at all, Truman. Not one scrap of it. This idea isn't any stranger than what we all know is happening. Maybe right now."

Truman shrugged his shoulder, agreeing with them.

"But we do know that something is doing this. Therefore, it has to be something close to town. There's not much else around here, Truman. It only makes sense."

"It's not an animal," Ebby began. "We'd have seen it. Whatever this is, it hasn't even been seen. That means it's smart, like a human."

"And," Jerry said with a grin, "While I do admit that being smart rules out half the people in town, it can't be anything but humanoid."

"Humanoid? Jesus. Y'all sound like some science fiction nerds on one of those big foot shows."

"Honestly, tell us what you think it is then," Ebby replied.

Truman threw his hands up and let them drop. "I haven't the faintest clue."

"Really?" Jerry asked. "You're as close to this stuff as anybody. You see the crime scenes and what it can do. And you've not come up with one thought of what it might be?"

"You're right. I've seen the bodies. It ain't a pretty sight. The reason I can't believe it's a human like y'all say is because no human would do what this thing does." Truman closed his eyes and shook his head. "The sheer rage on display is…I can't even describe it. This thing is a monster."

"It being a vampire just makes sense. I'm not talking about some teenage romance vampire from the movies, Truman. That's not what they really are. Like you said, they're monsters."

"And?" Truman asked.

"If it is a vampire, that means it has to be somebody in town, like we said."

"You ever consider that it lives in the woods?"

Jerry shook his head. "That's not how they operate. They look like normal people when they want to. They're monsters, Truman. Not wild beasts."

"Just find the nearest castle on top of a hill, and you'll have your man."

"That's movie crap. They're just normal people. Almost."

"Well, if they're normal people, they've got y'all beat." Truman turned and walked back to the door. "I don't want to hear a word of this around town, guys. Seriously. You know how people are. Before you know it, some idiot will have somebody tied to a stake and set on fire in the middle of town. We'll have truckloads of redneck idiots with guns marauding through town. One word of this, and it'll get real bad real quick. That I can guarantee."

"We're not telling anybody, Truman. I promise. We just told you because we know you, and you're a cop."

"Well, I'm not a cop anymore. I resigned today, so it's none of my business anyway."

"Resigned? Why?" Ebby gasped.

"I just need a change." Truman walked to the door. "Like you said, I'm as close to this crap as anybody. I'm tired of it. Please, don't get anybody hurt with this mess. Okay?"

"You mean like the tons of innocent people that's already been hurt and killed by this thing?" Jerry asked.

Truman looked between his two friends and, without a response, turned and left the room. The ember of guilt that he'd always felt began to ignite. He understood all too well what Anthony Swails felt because the entire force felt it. They were cops, they were supposed to do something, but they were as helpless as everyone else.

He pushed a hand through his hair as he made the second-floor landing. Turning, he worked his way down the steps to the lobby, thinking that he'd have been better off just staying in his room.

CHAPTER FOURTEEN

June 4th. Kill Day. Evening

Truman climbed onto the stool with a tired sigh and stood his flashlight on the bar. Gregg slid a bourbon and coke in front of him before he could order.

"Thanks. Do I look like I need a drink that bad?"

"Doesn't everybody? Tonight, at least."

Truman shrugged. It was true enough, but his troubles were closer to home than usual. He didn't feel like drinking but lifted the glass anyway.

The liquor went down warm, blossoming in his stomach. Truman closed his eyes and sighed, letting the alcohol begin its work. He'd felt like this was going to be a bad year, and so far, it was living up to his prediction.

"I gotta tell you, man," Gregg began as he wiped the bar with a towel. "There's a weird vibe this year. Know what I mean?"

Truman shrugged again. "Isn't there a bad vibe every year about this time?"

"Yeah, but it feels different this year." Gregg hung the towel over his shoulder and leaned on the bar. "I've lived here all my life. I remember we used to hide in my grandfather's storm cellar. I hated it. I can still smell the dirt and Liniment. He also used it as a root cellar. You know, to this day, I can't even get a whiff of sweet potatoes without a knot forming in my gut."

"Sounds like a blast," Truman said, uninterested. He took a long sip of his drink. When he sat it down, he watched his fingertip caress the top of the glass. "This shit is just insane if you ask me. The whole thing. Just freaking crazy."

"You're just figuring this out?" Gregg asked with a chuckle. "I mean, it's always been this way, so most folks don't know anything different. I guess it's part of our collective psyche, you know. It's who we are. Some towns have good football teams or a waterpark. We've got this. We just don't advertise it."

"That's just it. We didn't choose this. Hell, we don't even know when this started."

Gregg shook his head. "I'm no help there. My grandfather didn't either, and he was super old when he died. Hell, maybe it's always been this way from the beginning of time."

Truman let out a sarcastic chuckle. "That's just it. Why hasn't anyone ever gone to the feds? I mean, I know the mayor can't do it, officially. They'd think he was nuts. But you'd think a civilian would have called the National Guard or something."

"Yeah, I'd like to hear that call. Hello, Governor Baskin, this is Joe Nobody. See, there's this thing killing folks down here in our piss ant town in the far-flung woods of Hillburn County. Friendly, yeah. That's the place. I know you're busy, but can you send some troops down? What? Oh, no, we don't know what it is. No. Nobody's ever seen it. Yeah, we just find dead bodies every June Fifth. Uh, yeah, we've done it for years and never told anybody. Sorry. Now, about those soldiers…"

Truman nodded and sighed again. "Maybe you're right." He rubbed his forehead. "When I first married Megan and moved here, she told me everything. Naturally, as any sane man would, I didn't believe a word of it. I thought it was just a legend or something, you know. So I humored her and put up the plywood. Sealed the house up tight. We drank cheap wine from a box and played checkers by candlelight. It was kinda nice. Like a vacation. We got drunk and screwed each other's brains out. All in all, it was a pretty damned good night."

"Until daybreak," Gregg said.

Truman nodded. "Yup. The Chief came by in a truck at daylight. I was tired and hungover. His wife had made everyone sausage biscuits. Can you believe that?"

Greg shrugged. "We're southern. That's what we do in times of crisis. We feed people."

Truman nodded. Greg wasn't wrong. "Anyway, I was still thinking it was a joke. I ate two of those biscuits on the way to the first house. I took one look inside and puked up both of them all over the porch."

Gregg shook his head. "Yeah, you guys got it rough. Is it as bad as they say?"

Truman's hand stopped with the drink inches from his lips. "Yes, it is." He took a gulp of the drink and sat it down. "The house was out on Red Clay Road. Nice little ranch. Big ole rose bushes in the yard in full bloom. They were pink. From the road, it looked like a normal house. The grass was cut. There was a swing on the porch. It was nice, but a hole had been torn in the back."

"Kinda makes you wonder about the plywood on the windows, huh?"

Truman chuckled. "That it does. I guess it just gives people a sense of security, like when a hurricane is coming, you know. Maybe it keeps the light down. Hell, maybe it just gives people something to do with all the nervous energy."

"I guess." Gregg pulled the towel off his shoulder and went back to wiping. "I joke that Scott Handley got that started so he could sell the same plywood to the same people every year."

Truman shrugged. "Anyway, the whole place was torn to hell and back. It looked like a freaking bomb had gone off. There was an old man in the living room. He'd been torn to shit. He had a hunting rifle but never got a shot off. I'll never forget how white he was. He was like a ghost."

Gregg screwed up his face. "Damn."

"Anyway. I never made light of it again. We cleaned up two bodies that day. People acted like it was a win. Only two dead."

"Sometimes there's just one."

"One would be too many if it was your family."

Gregg nodded in agreement. "It's just me and an old hound dog, but I get what you're saying. Some years, there are four or five. I guess one or two is an acceptable loss, all things considered."

"Still." Truman's eyes moved past Gregg to the rows of liquor bottles sitting on shelves against the back wall of the liquor cabinet. His head tilted to one side, and his brow furrowed in thought. He looked back to Kevin and asked, "Why doesn't this bar have mirrors back there?"

Gregg turned and looked at the cabinet. Turning back to Truman, he shrugged. "Hell, if I know. The boss is old school, I guess. Maybe he doesn't like the way he looks."

"It's kinda odd, don't you think?"

"You know, different strokes and all that. Funny thing, people assume that the mirrors are to make it look like you got lots of liquor, but actually, it's from the old days. Those saloons could be a rough place, and people sitting at the bar with their backs to the door wanted to see who came in."

"Yeah?" Truman asked, his mind going back to Jean. "That makes sense, I guess. It's still odd, though."

"A little. To me, the mirrors kinda make the place look cheap, though. This is a swanky hotel. Folks probably don't have to worry about people sneaking up behind them."

Truman nodded in agreement. Like every other argument

running through his head, there was a reasonable explanation for this one, too. He finished his drink and pushed the glass over to Gregg.

"Another?"

"No. I better not. I'm going to try to get some sleep."

Gregg looked over the room. Three small groups were still gathered around tables, talking quietly. "Looks like I'll be up a while."

"Do me a favor, will ya?" Truman asked as he stood. "Don't let anybody get too drunk. The last thing I want to deal with is a fight or some drunk knocking on people's doors in the middle of the night."

Gregg nodded. "Hey," he said, catching Truman as he turned to leave. When Truman turned back, he asked, "What do you think it is?"

"What?"

"The creature. What do you think it is?"

"Oh," Truman shrugged, doing his best to be dismissive. "I don't have a clue."

Gregg looked around, then leaned over the bar. "Do the police know something? Is it really a vampire?"

"We know as much as anybody else does." He thought of Jerry and Ebby's map. "Probably less."

"C'mon, man. Is it a vampire or not?"

"I haven't the faintest idea. Really."

Gregg nodded, smiling. "I bet it's just like in the movies. Probably some smoking hot chick. Kinda odd, but one that every guy in town wants to bang."

"I seriously doubt that," Truman said with a laugh. "First of all, there are no such things as vampires. That's all fiction, man. C'mon. This ain't Hollywood. And second, there's nothing beautiful about this thing."

"Sometimes the truth is stranger than fiction."

"And sometimes it's not."

Gregg nodded. "Yeah. I guess so."

"Look, I'm tired. Today has really kicked my ass. You have to take anything I say with a grain of salt, man. It's been a hell of a day."

"Yeah, sure. No problem."

Truman forced a smile and knocked on the bar. "Have a good night." He grabbed his flashlight and walked away.

"You too," Gregg said, watching Truman as he switched on his light. "Be safe."

Truman threw up his hand as he made it to the lobby. He turned and started up the steps without looking back, not wanting to know if Gregg was still watching him.

Ebby and Jerry's suspicions had planted an idea that he didn't like. Gregg's talk of the creature being beautiful had led his mind to Andrea, which in turn led him back to Jean, one of Jerry and Ebby's suspects.

His boots suddenly felt like lead weights as he plodded slowly up the grand staircase, a circle of light showing him the way. The liquor had taken the edge off his nerves, but his mind still raged with an argument. There was no way Andrea could have anything to do with this mess.

In the span of minutes, two different people had raised questions about three of the most important people in his life. The Chief, Jean, and though indirectly, Andrea. The whole idea sounded crazy. People were just stressed and bored. That's all it was. After all, vampires didn't exist.

There was no way Andrea could be involved. She was kind and accommodating. The hotel enjoyed a long list of five-star reviews, many of them mentioning Andrea by name and raving over her hospitality. She was beautiful and kind. She'd never be a party to something like this.

Yet, a small voice of doubt in the back of his mind persisted.

Feeling bad and needing to lie down did provide the perfect cover for Jean. Especially tonight, of all nights. But then again, he was old, and he worked hard. The hotel was full. He was stressed. Of course, he was tired during the sequester. At any other time, the hotel was mostly empty.

Sneaking through the small crack in his adamant refusal to accept the possibility, a sliver of doubt opened the floodgates of questions.

Andrea was very secretive, often disappearing for days. Maybe she was tending to Jean. She had been acting strange today. Jean did hail from Eastern Europe. That was no secret. Ebby's claim that he might be from Transylvania echoed through Truman's mind. Was Transylvania even a real place? Did it really exist, or was it a Hollywood thing too? He made a mental note to look it up.

It would explain why Andrea refused to let their relationship go further than an occasional affair, why she kept him at a distance. Was she hiding something? Was she protecting Jean?

Truman made the second-floor landing and switched the light off. It was getting late, and most of the guests were settling in, which was a good thing. He'd rather not see anybody right now. Especially since his visit with old friends had turned sour.

Grabbing the massive mule post, he rounded it to the steps leading to the third-floor, and his thoughts returned to Andrea. What if it was Jean? Could he turn him in? Could he kill him if it came to that? He didn't even know some of the people who died, and none of the ones he did know were close friends. But he loved Andrea. That was the one thing he was certain of, and turning Jean in would implicate her as well. She'd be ruined and would have to leave town.

Reaching the third-floor landing, he stopped and switched his light on, shining it down the hall. Every door was closed, including Andrea's. He considered going to it and knocking but didn't know what he'd say if she answered. This new train of thought had him out of sorts.

He peered down the hallway, wondering if the creature that had plagued this town for so long could have lived mere feet from him. If it were so, how could he not have seen it? How could he have been so oblivious?

He knew the answer. It was because of Andrea. He liked Jean, but he was secondary in his life to his daughter. His attention had always been on Andrea. Was that part of the plan all along? Was their relationship just a ruse?

He took a step toward her door, then stopped. He shook his head. He wasn't thinking straight. All of this vampire talk had rattled him. It was just plain crazy. It would all go away in a few days. He just had to weather the storm tonight.

CHAPTER FIFTEEN

June 4th. Kill Day, Evening

Truman's feet were moving before he was fully aware of what he intended to do. Before him, the light was trained on the doors at the far end of the hall. One was Andrea's. The other was Jean's.

He could put all of this nonsense to rest with a simple check. He could just open Jean's door and see if he was in bed. If he found a sick old man, all this talk of vampires would vanish. More importantly, any involvement Andrea might have would vanish with it.

What would happen if Andrea was in Jean's room? How would he explain the intrusion? She'd know something was wrong, and if she'd somehow heard his conversation with Ebby and Jerry, she would know he suspected her father of something unspeakable.

But what if he's not there?

Truman's gut knotted with the question, and fear rose in his chest. Worse yet, what if he was and he was the creature? He might walk in on something that he didn't want to. Would Jean kill him, too?

Halfway down the hall, Truman paused in the dark. Watching the circle of light on Jean's door, he became aware that his hand was shaking. He didn't have his service gun. All he had was the flashlight in his hand. Neither would do much against the creature, but he'd still rather have his gun.

But could he use it? Even if he found Jean in full monster mode, could he shoot the man who'd shown him nothing but kindness? Could he shoot the father of the woman he loved? If he opened the door and found the creature, one of them would have to die tonight.

You're not a cop anymore, Truman, he told himself. You don't have to worry about any of this anymore.

He spun with the light, intent to go to his room, but collided with a body approaching him from the opposite direction. His hands instinctively reached out, steadying them as he apologized. He brought the light up enough to illuminate the face of the person and gasped when he saw her.

"Andrea?" Truman offered a nervous smile. Her hair was windblown, and her pupils were dilated wildly.

"Truman?" She pushed a hand over her tangled hair.

"I was just, uh. Just headed in and thought I'd see if you were up," he said, unable to keep his eyes from washing over her. She wore a loose gray skirt that ended just below the knee and a white blouse that hung untucked. On her feet were a pair of low-slung flats.

"Is everything okay? You seem a little flustered."

"It has been a long and demanding day. The hotel is full, and a customer had a plumbing issue that took an hour to fix," she said with a sigh. "They were not happy." She shook her head, smoothing her hair again.

"I guess not. I'd figure most of them are asleep, or at least in bed."

"If only."

Truman cleared his throat, hating the sliver of distance that the ridiculous ideas had brought between them. Half of him wanted to grab her and kiss her beautiful lips, to carry her to his bedroom and be with her. The other half, the part that he despised, wondered if she could be hiding a killer.

"How's Jean?" he finally asked, breaking the awkward silence that fell on them.

"He will be fine. He's resting," Andrea said, motioning toward the staircase. "He goes up and down the stairs like a young man, but I'm afraid he's overdone it this year. He's old. People can be very demanding sometimes."

"I'm sorry to hear that. Anything I can help with?" Truman asked. His eyes dropped to her hands, clutched nervously in front of her skirt. "Maybe a visit would lift his spirits."

"No," she said quickly. "I'm sure he is sleeping." Her eyes searched Truman's face in the dim light. "It's nothing I can't handle."

"Well, maybe he'll get plenty of rest tonight."

"I'm sure he will," she said curiously, her brow furrowing as she looked at him. "Were you going to check on us?"

"Uh," Truman looked back at Jean's door and then at Andrea. "I was. I mean, if a light was still on, I was."

Andrea shook her head. "It's late. He is sleeping. I told you he was ill." Andrea's eyes darted to Jean's closed door, then back to Truman.

"Look," Truman finally said, sensing her suspicion. "I was really hoping just to catch you. I couldn't sleep and was hoping to see you."

Andrea smiled, her face softening as she nodded.

"I didn't hear you coming up the stairs. So, uh, did you go to the wrong room?" he asked.

"What?" she asked, confused.

"Were you coming from my room?"

"I was, actually. I considered seeing if you were still awake."

"Oh?" Tuman asked, smiling despite his reservations.

"Well, I am. Still awake, I mean."

"But then I reconsidered."

"Oh," he said again, deflated.

"May I ask you something? Do you have friends in the hotel?" Andrea asked.

"Yeah. A couple from when I was married before."

"Ah," she said, nodding. "I see."

"Why do you ask?"

"One of the stewards said someone asked after you."

"It was probably them," Truman said, groaning internally. Had she heard the stupid conversation he'd had with Ebby and Jerry? Why else would she ask about them?

"Well," she said, her voice cracking slightly. She cleared her throat. "Goodnight then."

Truman stopped her as she tried to pass. Her body tensed beneath his grasp. "Are you okay?"

"Me?" She offered a smile, but the deep sadness in her eyes was clear even in the dim light. "I am fine, but you seem a little out of sorts this evening. Perhaps I should ask you the same thing."

"Nah," Truman lied. "I'm okay."

Andrea looked at him. Nodding. "I know what tonight is and, knowing who you are, I know it must be a bad night for you. Tasked with protecting the people from something that you couldn't possibly stop. It must put you in a difficult position."

"I suppose you're right." He turned to face her. The news of his resignation was on the tip of his tongue, but he didn't share it. "I just wish it was over."

"As does everyone, I'm sure. It is a difficult time of year for all of us."

Truman examined Andrea's face, hoping for a clue as to what she was thinking. Her demeanor was suddenly cold toward him, and he wanted to know why. If she'd overheard his friends, she might be hurt or angry, and she'd have every right to be. Once again, he cursed Ebby and Jerry and their stupid map.

As he stared at her. Seeing her vulnerable for the first time, his heart swelled with a mix of emotions. He wanted to protect her, to make her feel better. He wanted to be with her as badly as he ever had despite his concerns about Jean.

"I would like to see you tonight," he whispered.

"Would you really?" she asked, a hint of a smile coming to her face.

"I would. Very much."

She looked at him, a decision hanging in her eyes. Finally, her shoulders drooped, and she sighed quietly. "I'm afraid that it has been a very long day for us both, and with Papa not well, I've been very busy."

"Yeah," Truman said, internalizing his disappointment. "I understand."

"I think I would like to take a long hot bath and go to bed." Her eyes dropped to her hands. "Alone."

"Yeah, that's good. I'm sure you're tired. I'm tired, too. Maybe I'll turn in myself."

"Yeah," she said, offering a weak smile. "I guess this is goodnight then."

Truman watched her eyes search his and found a sadness in them that he'd never seen before. There was a finality within her look, like something was ending.

"Are we okay?" he asked quietly.

She drew in a deep breath and exhaled slowly. "Perhaps," she said with a shrug. "But only time will answer that."

Truman watched the sway of her hips as she walked away from him and moaned quietly, longing to be with her. She'd always been aloof and mysterious, but there was something about her voice that made his heart ache for her. He stood in the darkness and watched her until she passed the door to her father's room. When she was nothing but a shadow in the dark hallway, he turned toward his own room.

"You know," she said, her voice coming back to him from the gloom.

He turned, the light in his hand sending a soft glow down the hall after her. His heart skipped as she slipped her blouse over her head and held it in one outstretched hand.

Without looking back, she dropped the blouse to the floor outside her own door. "I do have a very large tub."

CHAPTER SIXTEEN

June 4th. Kill Day. Late

Truman looked at Andrea and smiled. Sitting opposite him in the tub, her hair in a loose knot on top of her head, the soft glow of the battery lamp highlighted her smooth, gentle features. She looked so much like a perfect lady from an old movie. Regal. Sophisticated.

His eyes washed down her neck to the mounds of her breasts, just breaking the surface of the bubbles, and a warmth spread in his stomach. It wasn't simple lust. The half-hour of frantic lovemaking they'd just had satisfied him and then some. It was so much more than that.

There wasn't a part of her that he didn't think was perfect. It was as if she'd been sculpted by an artist, each delicate curve made just for him to cherish. He loved the way she moved, the way she talked. The way she looked at him, her eyes roving his face. The urgency of her seeking made him want to kiss her every time.

All his suspicions had been vanquished with a simple word from her. There was no way the woman before him could be anything other than what he saw. Her father was old, the hotel was full, and his friends were stupid. It was that simple.

"Are you okay?" she asked. Lifting her glass of white

wine, her eyes danced over him over the rim as she drank.

"I am," he said with a smile as he lifted her foot out of the water. It was as smooth and perfect as the rest of her. Dragging his fingertip across the top, he found a tiny freckle and smiled.

"Because you're looking at me in a peculiar way."

"No, I'm not," he said. "You're looking at me in a peculiar way."

"I do not think so," she said with a laugh.

"Oh, I think you are," he whispered. Bringing her foot to his lips, he kissed the freckle.

She moaned quietly as his lips moved to the tips of her toes. "It's definitely you."

"Well," he said. "I can't help myself."

She smiled and put the glass aside. "Why do you like me so, Truman Malone?"

"What's not to like?" He kissed her big toe. "You're smart." He kissed another toe. "Beautiful." Another. "Strong." Another. "Resourceful."

"I may run out of toes before you run out of adjectives, but I like it."

"Well then, I may have to start kissing other things."

Andrea pulled her right foot from his hand and offered her left, smiling when Truman took it in his hands and gently wiped suds from it.

"Sexy," he said and kissed the first toe of her left foot. "Beautiful."

"You already said that."

"I know. But you're twice as beautiful."

Andrea drew in a deep breath and sighed. Closing her eyes, she laid her head back on the tile. "How do you see all those things in me when I cannot see any of them in myself?"

Truman shrugged as his fingers danced along the top of her foot and started up her leg. "That's just what I see when I see you. Every single time."

"Do you ever wish that a moment would last forever?" she asked, almost in a whisper.

"Yes. To be honest, almost every second I'm with you, I think that."

Andrea sighed, closing her eyes. "Nothing of the outside world. Only you and I and this tub exist. Beyond these walls, there are miles and miles of nothingness. Impenetrable darkness that insulates us from everybody and everything in the entire world. No duties, no responsibilities. Just nothing."

"If only that were true."

She sipped her wine and opened her eyes before setting it aside. "Would you like it to be true?" she asked, her eyes searching his.

"Wherever I am, if you are there, that's where I want to be."

"Before, when you asked if I was jealous of the woman you went on four dates with…"

"Yes?"

"I was terribly jealous. I am jealous. I'm jealous of every woman you've ever been with. I'm jealous that I was not them."

"No," Truman whispered as his hand caressed the top of her foot. "Every second of every day was wasted because I wasn't with you."

"Did you not love your wife?"

Truman planted a long kiss on the top of Andrea's foot. "I did at the time or thought I did. But now…" He trailed off, shaking his head.

"And now?" she asked.

"Now I know what a fool I was. If I could go back and spend all those years with you, I would do it in an instant."

"Time does not move backward, Truman. Only forward." She sighed. "Eternally forward."

"Well then, I want to make up for the time we've lost."

A pained smile came to her lips. "All this talk of time…" She shook her head gently.

Truman kissed the ball of her foot. "You have to know that I've fallen madly in love with you."

Andrea snatched her foot from his hand and sat up with a groan.

"What?" Truman asked, surprised.

"Why do you have to say that?"

"I don't know. What? That I love you? Can't you tell?"

Andrea looked at the ceiling and sighed again. "I'm sorry. It's my fault. We've been together too often lately, and I've led you on. I am sorry."

"Wait, please," Truman said, stopping her as she moved to get out of the tub. When she relented and settled back into the suds, he took her hands in his. "I'm sorry. I know you aren't looking for that, but I…" Truman pushed a hand through his hair. "You just…I'm fifty years old, and you make me feel like a schoolboy."

"Truman."

"Look, I'm sorry. I shouldn't have said anything."

"That's not it," she sighed, shaking her head. "My life is complicated. I have to care for Papa. There is no one else who can do it. It takes a great deal of time and energy. He isn't as well as you think. Then there's the hotel to look after. There's too much that you don't know about me for you to love me."

"I'd like to have the time to find out."

"Time," she said with a grunt. Closing her eyes, she shook her head again.

Truman put a hand along her cheek, his thumb caressing her skin. "What's wrong?"

"Nothing's wrong," she said, forcing a smile despite her misty eyes. "You're a good man, Truman. You deserve to have a woman who can spend the rest of her life with you."

"That could be you. I want it to be you."

She looked at him, then dropped her gaze. She closed her eyes and sighed. Opening her eyes, she lifted her hand, watching the suds and water slide from her palm. "I must confess that I would like that very much."

"Then what's the problem?"

"Oh, Truman," she sighed. "You said it yourself. Time passes, and people change. Do you not admit that although we've been together many times, you barely know me."

"I know enough to know that you're the woman I want to be with."

"What if I become difficult or fall ill? Will you still have that look in your eye?"

"I'm sure I would."

"But you do not know so." Andrea smiled.

"Look, why don't we just worry about tonight? Forget I said anything," he begged.

"Is this such a shallow thing between us that it cannot withstand a difficult talk? The slightest of troubles?"

"All I know is that I want to be with you every second of every day. That I am sure of. I want to smell your perfume on my sheets and feel the warmth of your body next to me in the night. I want to watch your eyelids get heavy as you fall asleep and hear you yawn like a child in the morning when you wake up."

She reached out and laid a palm along his cheek. "You are a good man, Truman."

"And you're a good woman."

Andrea grunted softly. "That is debatable."

"I don't think it is. Not even a little bit."

"You say that you love me, but you only know the me that I choose to show you."

"I see more of you than you think."

"Truman, I need to go. I must check on Papa and make the rounds. People probably need things from me."

"What if I need you?"

"You don't need me, Truman. You want me, and I appreciate that. But you do not need me."

Truman took a deep breath as he stared at their hands. Looking up at her, he smiled. "If I walk into a room you've just been in, my soul can feel it, and it makes me happy. Just knowing you're here, in this hotel, makes my heart happier. Last year you left a pair of your shoes in my room, and I was glad to have them there because they were yours. When you found them and took them away, I missed seeing them. That's how I feel about you."

"I must go. I'm sorry." She pushed up from the tub and grabbed a towel, covering her front side as she stepped onto the mat. Truman's eyes followed, gasping when he saw her back.

Lines of scars, long healed, began just below her shoulder blades and extended to just above the curve of her hips. Each one six to eight inches long, they lay across her porcelain skin like angry pink fingers, some of them overlapping.

He'd been a cop for a long time and had seen plenty of scars. He even had some of his own, and he knew that to leave a scar this pronounced after such a long time, the initial wound had to have been excruciating.

"Your back," he whispered.

"See," she said, pausing to look over her shoulder at him. "There's much about me that you don't know."

Truman watched her walk from the room, his eyes locked on her back. It looked as if she'd been whipped badly as a child. But by who? Surely not Jean. He got up to go after her, but the door to her room slammed, telling him she was already gone.

He sighed and grabbed a towel of his own, his mind reeling. He'd seen her back many times, but there were no scars on it before. He'd have noticed something like that, even in the throes of passion. They weren't fresh, but they were obvious. There was no way he hadn't seen them, felt them before.

Unless they weren't there.

New suspicions charged forward in his mind again, and his knees weakened. He sat down hard on the edge of the tub. Had she hidden them somehow? Could she do that? If so, why would she reveal them now? Was she a shapeshifter of some sort? Could she mask her true self? If so, what the hell had he been making love to all this time?

Ebby's voice came to him again. "Everybody knows vampires look like normal people when they're not hunting."

Was that it? Was *she* the creature instead of Jean? His stomach knotted at the possibility. "No," he said, his voice echoing back to him in the empty room. "No."

Andrea was right. There was much that he didn't know about her, but now he was determined to find out all that he didn't know.

Exiting the bathroom wrapped in a towel, he called for her, knowing she wasn't there. He lifted the lamp, illuminating her room. The bed along the far wall was still a mess from their earlier activities, but the rest of the room was immaculate. And empty.

He looked around, throwing one hand up and letting it drop to his side with an exasperated sigh. Now, what was he going to do? Standing in the bathroom door, he considered staying here and waiting her out. She'd have to come back sometime.

Deciding against it, he sat the lamp atop a chest of drawers and grabbed his clothes. He yanked his jeans over his wet legs and walked back to the lamp as he tugged his shirt over his head. One hand grabbed the lamp, and then he froze.

The light was falling on the painting on the wall at an odd angle, highlighting the texture of the brushstrokes. Encased with a thick black frame, each of the countless scallops of paint cast a tiny shadow, giving the impression of fish scales across the canvas. He lifted the lamp, moving closer to the painting.

The scene was the countryside at twilight. The look of the barn in the distance gave the impression of old-world Europe. The light of the rising full moon shone on the tops of the hills, illuminating piles of harvested wheat. Long shadows slipped down the canvas, blending with the darkness yet out of reach of the moon's glow.

His eyes roved over the scene and found a figure nearly hidden close to the bottom. The woman's long dress was barely a shade lighter than the dark paint, but her skin was pale. The look on her face struck him as sad, pained. It was the saddest painting he'd ever seen.

He pushed the light closer to the figure, discovering that the woman's long flowing hair was a deep auburn, like Andrea's.

He swallowed hard, his eyes locked on the woman. His head shook gently, refusing to accept the notion trying to surface in his mind. The woman in the picture couldn't be Andrea. She'd obviously purchased it, maybe because of the resemblance. Or her father. Maybe he'd bought it for that same reason.

Backing away from the picture, he held the lamp high. Looking around the room, he examined the other pieces of art adorning her walls. The paintings, four in total, looked old and dark, like the first. All were framed in the same dark, heavy wood. All of them featured a moon, though in different phases. Each of them contained the same woman as well. In every painting, she wore the same dark dress and the same sad look on her face. In two of them, she was close. Two, she was far, on a distant hill.

In one of the ones that portrayed her close, she was looking over her shoulder at something behind her. In the other, she was looking back at him. The woman in the painting had green, haunting eyes full of regret and sadness, loneliness.

Truman drew in a long, slow breath as his mind reeled,

trying to put pieces together that didn't want to fit. Her secrecy, the scars that suddenly appeared on her back, dark, haunting artwork. He'd always known there was something special about her, but could it be what he now feared?

No. Andrea was just into gothic art like countless other people. That didn't mean anything. He was no art connoisseur. For all he knew, the paintings could be priceless works. Highly sought after.

That didn't explain the scars, their odd meeting in the hallway, the things she'd been saying…

The sound of a breeze came to him, and he spun, catching movement by the window. Going to it, he drew the heavy drapes back to find a sheet of plywood painted like all the others in the hotel. He breathed a sigh of relief and was about to turn away when the wind gusted again, moving the curtain in his hand.

He pushed the drape further aside and gasped. The plywood was just leaning against the wall, and the window itself was open. "Holy shit," he whispered, looking around. There were three more windows in the room. He hurried to each of them, snatching the drapes back to find all of them just like the first.

"What the…" He looked around the room in shock while his mind threw questions at him like knives. Why didn't she board her windows? Didn't she know what danger she was in? Wasn't she worried about the creature?

The thoughts came to a screeching halt as a possibility swam into his mind. His eyes darted from artwork to artwork, absorbing the darkness within them. Her voice telling him that there were many things he didn't know about her echoed through his head as the image of her scarred back came back to him.

His former boss' voice broke into his mind. "There's never been an attack at the hotel."

"No," Truman said, silencing the voices in his head. It

couldn't be her. That meant it had to be Jean.

His mind showed him the image of Andrea's back again, and he pushed a hand through his hair. It couldn't be her. It couldn't be. He headed for the door, depositing the lamp in front of the painting.

CHAPTER SEVENTEEN

June Fifth. After midnight.

"Okay, okay. Chill out. Jesus, man."

Truman listened to the muffled complaints coming through the door with impatience. When Jerry opened it, he pushed inside quickly.

"Truman? What in the hell is wrong with you? What time is it?"

Truman held a flashlight up between him and Jerry. "I know it's late, but listen. I've been thinking about all that stuff you said before. About the vampires and stuff. I want some more information."

"What? Can't it wait, man? It's really late. We were asleep."

"What is it, Truman?" Ebby's came to them from the dark.

"Are you decent?" Truman asked.

"Descent enough if I don't have to get out of bed."

"You don't. I just need information." He went to the bed, leaving Jerry to complain in the darkness. "I've been thinking about this whole vampire thing—"

"And you think we're right," Abby said, wrapping the covers over her lower half as she sat up in the bed, an oversized tee shirt hanging on her shoulders.

"I think it makes as much sense as anything else."

"What changed your mind?" Jerry asked, joining his wife on the bed while Truman pulled up a chair. "Did you see it?"

"I didn't see anything. I've been stuck in this hotel like everyone else, and I couldn't sleep. Just say that I've been piecing together some clues, and I need information. All I know about the subject is what I've seen in movies. How accurate is that?"

Jerry shrugged. "Some are close, others not so much."

"Fair enough. Do they really feed off people? You know, drink blood and all that?"

"That seems to be the general consensus. Yes."

"What happens to people they feed off of?" Truman asked.

"It depends. First of all, there seem to be two schools of thought. One that if you're bitten, you become a vampire too. Some think that if you're bitten, you die."

"But that might be because of losing too much blood," Jerry added.

"But all the people around here were torn to hell and back. Why do that?" Truman asked, rubbing his chin.

Ebby scratched her head as she yawned. "Um. If I had to guess, it's to keep them from becoming vampires. Maybe?"

"It also could be because our guy is angry. This many victims in one area are a little out of the ordinary. Usually, vampires tend to wander or at least travel to feed. There might be something about this place that they just don't like and so they take it out on their victims. Or maybe they were slighted or something. There's really no way to tell."

"Or they like it here for some reason, but that's unlikely. They'd be risking being found out."

Truman rubbed his temples. "Are they solitary, or do they have families?"

"Again, that's debatable. I would say most are solitary or have some sort of companion that takes care of them. They don't marry and have children in the conventional sense."

"Why not?" Truman asked.

"According to lore, vampires are the undead. They live for thousands of years. I guess being with the same person that long kinda gets old." When Ebby cleared her throat, Jerry smiled and added, "Present company excluded, of course."

"I read something about a month ago," Ebby began, offering Jerry a smile. "It talked about the fact that they were undead, that they rarely feel any genuine emotion. And even if they did, it wouldn't be the same as we feel them."

Truman's shoulders slumped. Could it be true? Could Andrea have continued on with him without a shred of real emotion? He shook his head, unwilling to believe it. "What about this companion thing? Tell me about that."

"I guess they need looking after, or maybe protecting when they sleep."

Ebby nodded, agreeing with her husband. "I mean, when they're not a hideous monster, they're pretty normal, but I'm sure they are limited. Think of it like a personal aid."

"Like their slave?" Truman asked.

Ebby shrugged. "Maybe. I guess it depends on the situation."

"What's got into you, Truman? Earlier, you were dead set against all this."

"I know," Truman said with a sigh. "I just thought that as an officer of the law, I should investigate every angle. I couldn't sleep, so I got to thinking." He chewed on a thumbnail as his mind worked. "This whole emotion thing, it's not necessarily proven, is it? I mean, you said it tears up its victims because it might be angry. Anger is an emotion."

"True, but it's more innate, not like, say…compassion or love." Ebby raked a hand through her hair. "Are you sure you're alright? You look pretty shaken up. Did something happen?"

"No," Truman lied. "I told you. I've just been thinking,

and now I got all these questions." He shrugged, tossing up his hands at their inquisitive stares. "Look, sorry I woke y'all up. Go back to sleep. We'll talk about this more tomorrow."

"You know what?" Jerry asked, shaking his finger first at Ebby, then at Truman. "You've been locked up here like the rest of us. I think you know more than you're letting on. Do you think someone in the hotel—" He stopped when Ebby gasped.

"Is it Jean Ardelean?" she asked. She and Jerry exchanged wide-eyed looks. "Is it?" she asked again.

"What? No." Truman stood from the chair. "I told you I was just thinking about it."

"Did you see him?" Jerry asked eagerly.

"Jean's sick. He's been in bed most of the evening."

"That sounds like a good cover story if you ask me," Jerry said, drawing agreement from his wife.

"He's old. The hotel is full. He just overdid it, that's all."

"If you think about it, it makes perfect sense," Ebby said.

"No. It doesn't make any sense," Truman replied.

"There are only a few places that haven't had an attack. This hotel is one of them."

"Not true. There are hundreds of houses that haven't been hit. Also, the school and the Presbyterian church haven't been."

"Yes," Jerry said, ignoring Truman. "Don't dip your quill in the company ink. Bad for business."

"C'mon guys. Don't get yourselves all worked up for nothing. It's not Jean." Truman shook his head, regretting ever knocking on their door. "You're forgetting that they've only been here for about ten years."

"That is true," Ebby said, tapping her chin with her fingertip. "But, it doesn't rule him out. Remember? They travel to feed. Maybe he lived somewhere else."

"But why would he move here?" Truman asked, being careful not to implicate Andrea. Things were already bad enough.

"That is a good question," Jerry said, rubbing his palms together.

"Arrogance?" Ebby suggested. "Or maybe he's gotten too old to travel. Pretty nice set up here already."

"That's true," Jerry said, nodding. "Or maybe he was invited here by somebody."

"Guys. C'mon. Really?"

"Maybe somebody with influence," Ebby suggested.

"Like the Chief." Jerry pointed at Truman. "We had them both on our list." He extended a hand, high-fiving Ebby.

"Okay. I see now that this was a mistake. I have been around both those men for years and haven't noticed one thing out of the ordinary."

"Like what? Fangs and a cape?" Jerry asked, laughing. "If they were vampires, you'd never know it. "Think about it, man. All the things you guys have tried to stop it haven't worked."

"Remember all those motion camera thingies? Huh? Who better to avoid them than the man who helped put them up?"

"First of all," Truman began, holding up a finger. "We put them up, not the Chief. Best that I recall, he was in his office the whole time. And secondly, that was just a concession to the mayor. Nobody really thought it would work in the first place."

"Maybe he's one, too," Jerry said with a shrug.

"Okay. Now, this is getting out of hand. Jean, then the Chief, now the mayor. Who y'all going to accuse next? Me?"

"Don't be silly," Ebby said with a laugh.

"Dude, we know it's not you. We've known you for years."

"Well," Truman said, looking at Jerry. "I've known those men for years, and so have you. I just came here for some answers, not a witch hunt. Damn, guys."

"Whoa, whoa, whoa." Jerry sprang from the bed and stopped Truman as he headed for the door. "Please. Stay. Look, I know I get carried away. I'm sorry."

"Yeah. You came for answers. Let us help you," Ebby said from the bed.

Truman turned back to the room with a sigh. "Look, guys, all this stuff about vampires and all that is fine for you, but I'm still a cop, at least technically. I've been a cop for most of my life. I see things in black and white. Cause and effect. I have to say that all of this still sounds ridiculous to me. I'm sorry, but it does."

"Does the fact that a whole town sequesters once a year and allows this thing to just simply take two or three people make any more sense?" Jerry said, ushering him back to his seat. "I mean, just knowing what happens here every single year, year after year, pushes us beyond rational thought."

"He's right," Ebby added. "I mean, just the facts alone dictate the existence of something outside the realm of normalcy. Don't you think?"

Truman sat down in the chair again and rubbed his face with both hands. His hands dropped to his lap, and he shook his head. "All these years…" he trailed off.

"Officially, what do you guys think it is?" Jerry asked. Sitting down on the bed, he rested his elbows on his knees and leaned forward.

"That's just it," Truman said, tossing his hands up. "The Chief doesn't have an opinion. At least not one he's shared with us. I mean, he's as helpless as anyone else. I think he's just trying to mitigate the carnage, you know." Truman rubbed his eyes with his fingertips. "The mayor, and apparently most of the town council, think it's a vampire."

"Look, Truman, we know that it's something. This is a small town. People talk. We know that it does considerable damage to its victims and that it bleeds them out. That's a natural assumption."

"That's just it. Say we make that leap and say it's a vampire. Doesn't that open the door to everything? Trolls, elves, bigfoot, wendigos? I mean, every legend now becomes, or at least has the possibility of being real."

Ebby sighed. "That's a possibility. I guess."

Jerry shook his head. "You're thinking too existentially. Just because this thing is a vampire doesn't make every half-cocked theory true. To be honest, with a little detective work, most cases can be sorted out rather quickly."

"But it is something," Ebby insisted. "I mean, a regular person couldn't tear their way into a boarded-up house."

"Or drain other people of all their blood."

Truman rested his elbows on his knees and held his head in his hands with a heavy sigh. Staring down at the tennis shoes on his feet, he noticed that one of the laces on the right one was misaligned. He'd had the shoes for years and had never noticed it, but now he discovered it was obvious. His brow furrowed as he stared at it, baffled. How could he not have noticed before?

"I know all of this stuff; the map, us predicting who's going to get it next, all that stuff, seems incredibly morbid. I guess it is when you get down to it, but I guess it's just our way of coping. I don't know." Ebby sighed as Jerry took her hand. "But the fact is that something big and strong is doing all this. You know that more than anyone. You see what it can do. What it has done."

Truman raised his head to the ceiling, closing his eyes as a realization slowly dawned on him. Despite all his training and experience, something obvious could exist right under his nose without him ever noticing it. The possibility that Jean Ardelean could be the creature became very real. That meant Andrea was also involved somehow.

"Look," Jerry began. "At its core, if you strip away all the Hollywood bullcrap, a vampire is a soulless creature damned to roam the Earth with an endless lust for blood. What it looks like is probably unknowable because every time one reveals itself to someone, they die."

Truman stood on legs that didn't want to support him. His stomach was churning, and he felt sick. Looking between his friends, he swallowed hard. "Thanks, guys. Really. You've helped a lot. Do me a favor, though. Let's keep this conversation to ourselves."

"What are you going to do?"

Truman shook his head. "I don't know, but if one of the people you were talking about finds out we're on to them, all hell might break loose."

"Yeah," Jerry said, nodding. "That makes sense."

"Truman, be careful," Ebby said with a flat smile. "You know what this thing is capable of."

"Yeah." Jerry stood and put a hand on Truman's shoulder. "This sequester is almost over. You've got a year to figure things out. Don't do anything rash."

Truman nodded. Suddenly, nothing else mattered except finding Andrea. He had to see her. He had to know the truth.

"I think right now I need to go to bed. It's late, and I'm getting tired." He grabbed the light from the bedside table and staggered to the door. "I'll talk to y'all tomorrow. Get some sleep."

"You okay, buddy?" Jerry asked, walking him to the door. "You look like you just got punched in the gut."

Truman nodded and thanked him as he opened the door. "I'll be fine. Thanks. I just need some sleep." He stepped into the hallway, but Jerry grabbed his arm.

"Don't you want to know how to kill it?"

Truman's heart sank, the question hitting him like a punch. "Um. No. Not right now," he said, recovering. "There will be plenty of time for that later on. I'll, uh, I'll let you guys know what I find out. Okay? We'll talk about that then."

"Okay, man. Get some rest. You look pretty wrung out."

"I feel wrung out," Truman said and walked away, leaving

his friend in the dark. When the door closed behind him, he fell against the wall with a heavy sigh. His mind replayed the scene of Andrea getting out of the tub. The scars on her back were a definite sign of something, and the only way to find out was to find her.

CHAPTER EIGHTEEN

June 5th. Predawn.

Truman sat down hard on the bottom step of the grand stairway with an exhausted groan. He switched the light off and dropped it on the carpeted walkway next to him. His legs ached from walking, and he couldn't remember when he'd last eaten, not that he could keep anything down if he tried.

His stomach felt hollow, and there was a pain in his chest that he almost wished was a heart attack. So quickly, his whole world—a world that he thought he had a good grasp on—had been turned upside down. He had no job, and two people who had been staples in his life were embroiled in a scenario that was nothing short of unbelievable.

His head ached to the point of tears. His mind was a jumble of incoherent thoughts flip-flopping from one extreme to the other. Some time ago, he couldn't remember how long, it had slipped into a pattern of simply showing him alternating memories of Andrea and of the victims he'd collected through the years.

He saw her gentle laugh, her head tilting slightly. She turned and looked at him, her eyes vibrant and alive. She was happy. Then her face morphed into Harriet Weems' ghostly white features, her face locked in an agonizing, silent scream.

Another memory flashed into his mind. Andrea was walking ahead of him, then looked over her shoulder. One eyebrow was cocked seductively as she led him to her room. Her hair bounced with each step. A smile spread across her pink lips. She was beautiful. Then, in an instant, it changed to Howard Deal. He was lying prone on the floor of his bedroom, his head twisted to one side at an odd angle, his neck broken.

Truman grabbed the sides of his head, trying to make the images go away. Alone, sitting in the dark while everyone else slept, his tears finally came. For the first time in a long time, he didn't know what to do. He should investigate and try to find out the truth, but he feared what he might discover.

Had he gone too far already?

Despite everything, he still longed for Andrea. He always felt better when he was with her. If only he could find her, he could forget about everything. Ebby and Jerry's stupid map, the creature, the victims. They would all disappear.

He'd searched every inch of the hotel, again and again, hoping to find her. The only place he hadn't looked was Jean's room. He loathed knocking on the old man's door. If he was wrong about everything, he'd roust an old, sick man from his bed at an ungodly hour. If he was right, he might walk into the den of a killer.

Leaning against the mule post, he stared at the two oil lamps that flanked the front doors, still covered with sheets of plywood. The lamps had been trimmed low and now gave off very little light, resembling the dim, flickering eyes of some unseen giant.

During his frantic search, the rational side of his mind grappled with the possibility that he didn't want to face. Staring at the lamp closest to him, he remembered Andrea's face and the pain in her eyes as she looked back at him. And the scars on her back.

There is much you do not know about me.

Truman pushed a hand through his hair as her words once again haunted him. Was that an admission? His brain refused to accept it as one. She had to be protecting Jean. He was the monster. He was the one who'd beat her, scaring her back. That made more sense, anyway. It had to be Jean. Yes. Jean was the monster.

Then, she is his minder.

His mind conjured the images of last year's sequester, and he growled, pushing his hand through his hair again, trying to force them out. The gulf between the victims and the woman he loved was too great to cross. He refused to accept it. There was no way that Andrea was voluntarily a part of this.

Truman rubbed his eyes with the heels of his hands, pushing tears from the corners. He was tired of thinking about it, of thinking at all. His body begged for sleep, his mind for peace, but above all else, he simply wanted Andrea. He longed to hold her, to feel her breath on his cheek. He needed to feel her body against his, her voice in his ear.

His eyes went to the polished doors of the bar, watching as the dim flames danced in their shine. If the bar were open, he could get a bottle and drink it fast. That would shut his mind down, and he could pass out. It wouldn't solve anything, but at least he could stop thinking about it for a while. He could forget the horrible possibility and just sleep.

He could dream about Andrea, about her eyes, her lips. He could dream of her laugh and her voice as she called his name while they made love. He could dream of the smell of her perfume and the way her eyes darted around his face when she looked at him.

But the doors to the lounge were locked. Liquor would provide no respite tonight. He would have to make it through the night alone.

His hand climbed the mule post until his fingers found the top, digging into the ornate carvings. Pulling himself up, he looked up the dark stairway. So many times he'd traversed the steps, so many days a fool. Would things be different if he'd told Andrea how he felt sooner? Would it have ended sooner, sparing him this anguish, or would it have made things worse now? No, he decided. It couldn't get any worse.

As bad as the possibility of her aiding the creature was, the fact that they'd never be together again was equally painful. Though she'd eluded his hopes of a real relationship, he'd always held out hope that she'd change her mind. Maybe when Jean died, he'd told himself. Maybe next year. Maybe one day. Now, there were no more maybes.

Forcing his body to work, he bent with a groan and picked up the flashlight but didn't switch it on. Instead, he stumbled up the steps in the dark, each one taking more strength than the last. He'd knock on Jean's door and ask for Andrea. It was the last place she could be. If she wasn't there, he'd know it was over. He'd know that he'd lost her to whatever end may come.

One faint glimmer of hope remained, pushing him onward. Even if she aided him in some way, she wasn't the one who'd done the heinous things he'd seen. He'd confront Jean, tell him he knew. It was risky, but it was his only choice.

He would swear not to expose him and beg Jean to let him marry Andrea. They could go on as if nothing had happened. People would still die, but he didn't care anymore. He'd be with Andrea. They could take a vacation every June and pretend he knew nothing.

Truman made the second-story landing and switched the light on. The beam of light, weak from use, moved across a long, narrow table holding an elaborate floral display. He stared at it, trying to remember if it had been there all along. It was beautifully done, with long, graceful flowers billowing forth from a white porcelain vase that reminded him of Andrea herself.

He sighed deeply, the thought of her deflating him. Turning from the arrangement, he grabbed the massive mule post and rounded it to the steps leading to the third-floor. His mind replayed the first time he'd ever seen Andrea.

He was waiting in a chair that was tucked in the corner next to the dining room doors. Fresh from his divorce, he needed a temporary place to stay until he could sort things out. Sitting there, feeling like a failure because of his divorce, his choices were the Jupiter Hotel or a mobile home rental just south of town.

He looked up just as she rounded the staircase on the second-floor, and his heart began to race. Her hand was on the very post that his hands touched now.

Unable to look away, he watched her descend the stairs in what he'd come to know as her usual smooth, elegant way. Dressed in a green ankle-length dress that looked tailored to her body, she was demure and delicate, yet somehow defiant and strong at the same time. Her chin was high. Flowing red hair hung over her left shoulder. One slender arm extended to grace the handrail.

When she approached him with a smile, his heart missed a beat. When her green eyes fell on his, it stopped in his chest.

"Hello. I'm Andrea Ardelean," she said, her smile widening. "I've been told that you would like to stay with us."

Truman moaned. He was a veteran police officer, trained to notice things. How could he not have noticed what was happening right beneath his nose? Did he just not want to see it? Had his feelings for Andrea simply blinded him to the truth?

His mind stuttered, and he fell. Going to a knee, he clutched the railing. His body wanted to give in to his exhaustion and stay down. Mentally, he was spent. The only thing he'd wanted for almost ten years was within his grasp, yet out of reach at the same time.

Nearing tears, he drew in a deep breath to muster the energy and the will to pull himself back up. His thoughts on Andrea, his body on autopilot, he slowly worked his way up the steps. When he finally reached the third-floor, he stopped and fell against the wall. The light in his hand rose slowly, shining down the hall. Every door was closed, including hers. He considered going to it and knocking again but didn't know what he'd say if she answered. He moved the light to Jean's door and shook his head. In his condition, he couldn't bear another blow.

He drew in another deep breath and pushed off the wall. Turning, he headed toward his room. He took two unsteady steps and froze when a soft voice trickled down the hall behind him.

"You are so very troubled."

Truman didn't turn but absorbed the sound of Andrea's delicate voice as if it were a cool breeze. He closed his eyes and inhaled deeply as his chest grew with equal parts joy and fear. She was here, but what did she look like? She'd somehow hidden her scars from him. What else had she been hiding?

He swallowed hard and shook his head. He knew he had to turn to her. He couldn't not see her. He didn't have an ounce of proof that she'd done anything wrong. A few dark paintings. Some loose sheets of plywood. Scars on her back. None of them meant she was guilty of anything.

If Jean was the creature, she'd be equally innocent. She was his daughter, raised by a monster. What choice would she have but to help him?

Truman turned slowly, hoping with all his might that she would be herself. The light, dim in the distance, fell on her bare feet first. Feet that just hours ago he'd kissed. Beautiful, delicate feet, perfect like the rest of her.

He swallowed again and slowly lifted the light. It fell on her pale green bathrobe. He recognized it as the one the hotel supplied to its guests. When the light fell on her worried face, his apprehension collapsed. His body longed to run to her, but his legs wouldn't move.

"You are looking for me?" she asked pensively. Clutching her hands before her.

Truman nodded. "I am."

"Here I am," she said with a shrug, offering an apologetic smile.

Truman looked at her, and a smile escaped him. Even like this, fresh from the shower, her hair wrapped in a towel, she was a vision of beauty.

"I see."

Andrea dropped her eyes to her hands. When she looked back up at him, a tear clung to her cheek. "I think maybe we should discuss some things."

Truman fell against the wall as if punched. The sound of her voice spoke volumes. The look on her face told him that they'd spent their last night together.

"Will you come to me?" she asked, fighting back tears.

Truman nodded. "Always."

CHAPTER NINETEEN

June 5th. Predawn.

Walking the hallway felt like going to his execution. Along the way, all his questions became hands, grabbing at him, weakening his will. With each step, he grew closer to her, and maybe a truth he didn't want to know.

Truman hesitated, then closed the door behind Andrea as he followed her into her room. As soon as it closed, she turned to him, putting a hand along his cheeks. Her eyes were red, her cheeks tear-stained.

"You look very tired, my love."

"I am," he said, his voice barely escaping his throat. "I've been searching for you everywhere."

"You are worried and afraid. I'm so sorry."

Truman nodded. "I'm that too. But you don't need to apologize to me for anything."

Andrea's eyes frantically searched his face, darting back and forth as if she needed to see something. Her lip quivered when she found what she didn't want to see, and a tear rolled down her cheek.

"I just...I mean—"

"Shhh," she said, putting a finger to his lips. "Don't say anything yet. Please." She slid her arms around his waist and fell against him. "Will you just hold me for a while?"

Truman's heart swelled as he fought back tears of his own. His tired mind tried to protest, but the air was thick with her scent. He wrapped her in his arms and pulled her to him. There was no fear. He was in no danger from either her or Jean.

His thumb found the switch on the light and turned it off. He stood in the dark, enjoying the feel of her body against his, the smell of her. The heart racing in her chest beat against his. The thought of never holding her again hurt more than the truth that her eyes had confirmed.

After a long time, when her gentle weeping had subsided, he lifted her from his chest. Though he couldn't see her eyes in the darkness, he felt them on him. "You know that I love you like I've never loved anyone."

"Yes," she replied in a whisper. "That's why we must talk. You deserve to know the truth. All of the truths." She pulled away from him, leaving him in the dark. After a few seconds, the lamp he'd left by the painting came on, and light filled the room. She adjusted the knob, dimming it to the lowest level. She went to the bed and sat down, patting the covers beside her.

"Come. Sit with me, please."

Truman went to the bed and sat down. He wanted to know everything, and not at the same time. More than anything else, he wanted to be close to her.

"Will you do something for me?" she asked, unable to look at him.

"If I can." He thought for a moment, then nodded. "Yes. I will."

"Will you just listen for a while? Just let me talk. If you have questions, I will answer them, I promise. But I need to tell you my story first. It is long and not easy to tell."

"I'll listen to you as long as you need me to." He laid a hand along her cheek, thumbing away her tears.

"I'm not what you think I am." She sniffled and wiped her nose. "Well, maybe I am."

"Andrea."

"No. Please." She took his hand from her cheek and held it on her lap between hers. "If things were different." She shook her head, crying. "You're a good man, Truman, and I do love you. I've never allowed myself to say it, though I've known it for a long time. I really do, but I could never be the woman you need me to be."

Truman's heart sank as he watched Andrea struggle to find the words she wanted. He ached to relieve the pain she felt, though he knew he couldn't.

As she cried, anger rose in his chest, and he cursed those around him who had brought them to this desperate place. Damn, Ebby and Jerry and their fucking map. Damn, Gregg and his stupid questions. They were the ones who'd set all of this in motion. They'd got him to doubt her. If not for them, he could have gone on for the rest of his life, blissfully ignorant and loving Andrea.

Damn the mayor, and Rhonda, and Benjamin Steely and his stupid party too. Damn the town itself and everybody in the whole stinking place. What did he owe this town that it should cost him the one thing he wanted above everything else?

His tired mind and body wanted nothing else but to lay with her, their naked bodies intertwined as they slept. He remembered what she'd said in the tub about them being surrounded by a vast nothingness and wanted it to be true. He could live the rest of his life in that bubble and be happy.

Andrea sniffled and coughed, fighting back sobs. Her pain was palpable. He could feel it seeping from her body. He'd never seen another person in such a way, and the fact that it was the woman he loved pained him to no end. When she coughed again, he stood.

"Please don't leave," she begged, her voice desperate and afraid.

"I'm not going anywhere." He stroked her head as she dropped her gaze back to her hands. Standing above her slumped form, his eyes went to the back of her robe, and the image of her scarred back leaped into his mind.

Truman closed his eyes, willing the memory away with what little strength he had left. "I was just going to get you a drink." He took the lamp and staggered to the bathroom. There was a glass next to the sink. He held it under the tap and turned it on. His reflection was too bad to look at, so his eyes wandered to the top of the mirror.

The green head of a push pin caught his attention. Instinctively, he looked to the other side of the mirror and found another one. This one still held a few loose black threads. He stared at it, wondering if they'd been there before. The loose threads seemed as if someone had torn the drape away quickly, as if they didn't want him to see it.

Cool water spilled over the glass and cascaded down his fingers, bringing his attention back to his task. He turned off the tap and drank some of the water. His eyes went back to the pin and the threads it held, but his mind wanted no more mysteries to solve. Lack of sleep and the stress of the past few days were catching up with him. If not for Andrea, he'd be passed out across his bed, oblivious to the world.

He watched himself rub his wet fingers over his face as her name danced through his mind. He closed his eyes and saw her face, smiling and happy. She'd run into him on the main staircase. He was going up. She was going down. She stopped and leaned against the railing. She pulled her hair over one shoulder as she spoke.

"Hello there," she'd said, a smile tugging at the corner of her lips.

"Hello, you."

"How was work?"

He'd said something nonchalant, dismissive.

"I was just on my way to the dining room. Care to join me?"

"I can't think of anything I'd rather do."

"Well, the meal isn't anything special," she said over her shoulder as she started down the steps.

"It wouldn't matter what they were serving."

She looked over her shoulder at him, and her smile widened. In her eyes, he saw true, unguarded emotion that made his knees go weak. He saw so many things in one glance, all of which settled in his heart. And though she'd never said it aloud, he saw true, genuine love.

Truman opened his eyes and stared at himself in the mirror. He drew in a deep breath and let it out slowly. Nodding, he finally made a decision.

CHAPTER TWENTY

June 5th. Dawn

Andrea took the glass of water from Truman and drank from it. When she'd had her fill, she sat it on the bedside table and clasped her hands on her lap. She pulled the towel from her head and dropped it to the floor at her feet. Running a hand through her wet hair, she sighed and began to tell her story.

"A long time ago, a very long time ago, my life was changed. I was just a child. Ten years old, perhaps. We lived in a small mountain village. Life was difficult but good. We had the things we needed. We had a small garden for vegetables, and my father hunted in the woods nearby. As a child, I never wanted to leave my village. To me, it was the perfect place to live. Then, one night, I heard a noise outside my window."

She sniffled again, and Truman grabbed a box of tissues from her bedside table. Andrea wiped her nose and continued.

"I knew better, but I was a curious child." A sad laugh escaped her. "I thought I saw Papa in the garden, so I snuck outside to see what he was doing. I never believed the tales that my parents told me. I thought they were just to scare me into being good. When I found the man in the garden, it wasn't Papa at all. I knew he was a stranger, but I was too frightened to scream.

"I had always imagined him as a hideous monster with

sharp teeth and blood dripping from his face. He was nothing like the monster people said he was. He was tall and very handsome."

When Truman put a hand on her back, hoping to comfort her, he felt her racing heart, the hitch in her breath as she inhaled.

Andrea shook her head and sighed. "He asked if he could come inside the house. Somehow, I managed to say no. Then he asked if I wanted to come with him. I was too frightened to speak, but I shook my head. He said that he lived in a castle and that I would like it. But again, I shook my head. He came to me, crossing the garden in an instant. Looking up at him, he looked like a giant. For a time, he just stood and stared at me like he was trying to come to a decision.

"Then he swept me into his arms as if I were a feather. I thought he was going to kiss me, but he didn't. He said, 'I'm sorry, my child,' and then I felt him bite my neck. It hurt, and I started to cry. After that, I felt very tired and fell asleep. My father found me in the garden the next morning.

"He said I was curled up, sleeping peacefully amidst the turnips. I didn't feel well, so he put me straight into bed. I slept all day and the night. The next morning, I felt a little better."

She spared Truman a glance, then dropped her eyes back to their hands as she kneaded the tissue. "I didn't know what had happened to me. I wondered if it was all a dream. I told Papa, but he said I should be quiet. He said it should be our secret and to never tell anyone what happened. That was the first time I saw my father cry.

Our secret lasted another day, and then my mother saw my neck. She knew straight away what had happened. My father tried to persuade her not to, but she said she was taking me to the priest in town. They argued. My father begged her not to, but Mother was adamant. Papa threatened her, but she was not persuaded. Mother said if the village found out they were hiding me, they'd be punished as well.

"The next morning, my mother woke me early. She fed me, then we prepared to leave. My Papa kneeled in front of me and hugged me very tightly for a long time. He said to never forget how much he loved me. He wiped tears from my cheek and kissed me."

Andrea wiped away her tears and shook her head. "My papa was a good man, and I never doubted how much he loved me. I never forgot how it felt to be loved by him." She looked at Truman and forced a smile. "I never felt that way again until you loved me."

"I do love you." Truman put an arm around her shoulders, but she shrugged it off.

"My mother pulled me from his arms. We walked for miles in silence. She held my hand but refused to answer any of my questions. My mother never said a word to me. She just prayed every step of the way."

Andrea drew a shuttered breath and continued. "The priest locked me in a dungeon. They told my mother it was for my own good. I stayed there for a long time, but I never saw my mother or father again.

"All day and all night, the monks came and chanted and said prayers for me. They prayed for my soul, but they fed me very little." She shook her head. "Every day, my pleas fell on deaf ears. I was so scared and hungry. Cold. I was always cold. I begged to go back home to my mother and father, but they ignored me. When I came to the bars, they stepped back, always beyond arms reach. They were afraid of a little girl, of me.

"I remember that they never looked directly at me either. Sometimes, they came close enough to douse me with water that had been blessed in the church."

Truman reached out and took her hand.

"They would stand and watch me out of the corner of their eyes, writing things down. I can still hear their quills scratching on the papers. Then they would leave as suddenly as they came, and I would be alone again." Andrea shook her head slowly. "The nights were so long. I was often too cold to sleep and always hungry. I cried until I fell asleep, huddled in a corner like a dog.

"In time, I got used to all these things, though I never understood them. I hadn't changed at all. I was the same little girl I'd always been. Then, one day, a man came. An important man. He was dressed in fancy red robes with a sash around his neck. He had a large hat on his head. The regular priests bowed to him, scurrying about his feet like rats.

"He came to the bars and looked right at me. His head bent from side to side as if he were examining a goose at the butcher's shop. His eyes held no emotion. He just kept looking at me. The other men would whisper things in his ear, and he would nod.

"That evening, he made the nuns feed me until I was full, and then they were instructed to bathe me and bring me to the church. I was glad to be clean and fed. They gave me a new dress because my old one was in tatters. One of them even brushed and pleated my hair. I was so happy. I thought things would be better now, that they might send me home. I couldn't remember being so happy." Andrea released Truman's hand and dug her fists into her eyes.

He rubbed her back when she began to sob again, but she stiffened, and he drew his hand back. "I'm so sorry."

"By this time, I may have been there for a year. They took me to the man's chambers and tossed me on the floor at his feet. He was sitting on a big chair, just looking down at me like I was a rat in the sewer. I didn't know who he was or what to do, so I stood up. He came to me and slapped me so hard I fell to the ground again. He told me to never stand in his presence.

"I still remember the sound of his robe as he kneeled beside me while I was lying there crying. Suddenly, he grabbed my hair. He said the color of my hair was the reason I'd been picked and ordered my head to be shaved. The priests came and started cutting my hair. I tried to fight them, but they hit me. I stopped fighting. When they were done, my hair was no longer than a dog's. I felt so ashamed, but I didn't know why. I begged them to let me go home, but they refused. They said I was marked, that I was a monster. I tried to tell them that I was just a little girl. That I hadn't changed like they said I would."

Andrea covered her face with her hands. "I'll never forget the way they looked at me with such hatred, such malice. I wished I was dead."

"You were just a child."

Andrea shook her head slowly, lost in thought. "They kept me in a room in the church and went on with their chants for a long time, but nothing ever happened. I began to wonder what I was. The prayers and chants didn't work, so I knew God did not want me. But I didn't transform either, so the monster's power had also forsaken me. I was neither a child of God nor the devil."

Andrea sighed. Closing her eyes, she pushed tears down her cheeks. "Then, one day, they brought me to the man's chambers again. There was an alter set up, and they ordered me to kneel before it and renounce my evilness. I didn't know what that meant, so I prayed for forgiveness like my mother had taught me. I begged and cried and threw myself on the alter."

She opened her eyes, staring straight ahead. "But that wasn't good enough. They tied me to the damned thing and tore the back of my dress away." Andrea scoffed. "I was sad because they tore such a nice dress." She shook her head, her jaw clenching. "Then the man in the fancy robes hit me."

Truman drew in a sharp breath, realizing where the scars on her back came from.

"The pain was worse than anything I've ever known. I screamed until my throat burned, but he did it again. And again. And again."

A tear rolled down her cheek and collected on her jawline. It wavered as she drew in a breath, then dropped to her lap.

"I was out of my mind with pain. I only know now how many times he hit me because one day, I had Jean count the lashes. There are three times seven. Twenty-one. When he finally stopped, I was barely conscious."

Andrea pulled away from Truman and fell onto the bed. Covering her face with her hands, she broke into sobs. Her voice was uneven and weak when she continued.

"I was awake enough to feel what he did next. I felt a sharp pain and screamed. I tried to get away, but I was tied to the altar. He pushed no matter how much I cried out, how much I begged him to stop. He kept saying that I was a whore of the devil and that I deserved no less."

"My god," Truman gasped. His stomach knotted with disgust. "I'm so sorry."

"This continued for many days. I pleaded with the priests to release me or to kill me. I was so ashamed. I hated myself. I prayed for God to kill me, and I wondered what I had done to bring so much evil upon myself."

"None of that was your fault, Andrea. You have to know that now."

"I was an innocent little girl. I could barely read and couldn't yet write my own name. We were poor, and he was rich and powerful. It became clear that no one would ever stop him. Then…" She trailed off, nodding slowly. "Then, one day, I found a loose sliver of stone in my cell. I rubbed it against the floor until it was sharp on both sides. I sat in the dark with it against my throat for a very long time. I just wanted it to be over, but I couldn't do it. The next time they came to get me, I stabbed one of them in the chest. The other one ran away."

Andrea sat up abruptly, pushing Truman's hands away as he tried to embrace her. She angrily swiped tears from her cheeks with both hands.

"That's when I changed. When his warm blood ran down my arm, I could smell it as strong as freshly baked bread. The scent swept through me in an instant like a storm. I saw the fear in his eyes and felt his heartbeat as the blood left his body. I watched him die, and I liked it. I watched them all die that day. With each one, I grew stronger, and so did my desire for blood. That's when I became the monster that I am."

"No. Andrea, you're not a—"

"They hated me for what happened to me, an innocent child. To them, I was a monster to be reviled, beaten, abused. But I wasn't a monster. They are the ones who made me what I am."

"They were wrong. You're not a monster."

"Yes, in their treatment of me, they were wrong, but that doesn't change what I did. What I am."

Truman swallowed hard and drew in a long, unsteady breath. "It should."

"You will always see me as a monster now that you know the truth."

"Look, I don't even know what I'm feeling—"

"Stop!" she said, standing. "Right now, you don't know, but tomorrow you will. When you see what I've done. When you find the bodies, you will know it was me, and you will see me as a monster."

"Andrea, wait. I've left the—"

"No." She strode to the door and opened it. "I should never have told you. I should have left you with a few pleasant memories of me. Left you to wonder if it was really me."

"Why did you tell me this, show me the scars if you're just going to leave?"

"Because I was afraid that you would come to know the truth, and I wanted you to know why I am the way I am, that I'm not just a monster for the sake of bloodlust. My back, the scars, are just an ugly truth that I have hidden from you."

Truman came to her, took the door from her hand, and closed it. "Someone may hear you, Andrea." He shook his head. "Nothing about you is ugly, Andrea. Not even your scars."

"It doesn't matter anymore," she said, turning her face from him. "In the end, it doesn't matter why I'm a monster, does it? Just that I am one."

"You're not a monster." Truman tried to take her shoulders, but she resisted. He stared at her, struggling to reconcile the two truths he now knew.

"Am I not? You've been to the places I go, seen the things that I do." Her head spun to him, locking her eyes on his. "Tell me now that you don't think that is the work of a monster."

"Andrea…" He trailed off, shaking his head. Putting her and the scenes he'd witnessed through the years was like forcing opposite ends of a magnet together. His mind refused to make the connection.

"That's what I thought." She turned from him, taking a few steps away. "I suppose my misfortune was falling in love with one of the men who must clean up my messes."

"Look," he came to her. This time, she let his hands stay on her shoulders. "I do love you."

"Right here, right now, I believe that you mean what you say. But when the sun rises, and you collect the bodies, you will not. You will know I did these terrible things, and you will fear me, hate me."

"I know the truth now, and I don't hate you. Besides, I've—"

"You will," she said, pulling away again. "You will come to hate me."

"Look, I mean—" Truman shoved a hand through his hair, his mind afire with questions. "Can't you just stop? Just not do it?"

She gave him a contemptible laugh. "Can you stop breathing? Drinking water?" She shook her head. "I have no willingness to do these things, Truman. Don't you see that? Except for that day in the church, I never have. I did not choose this life." She closed her eyes and sighed. "There is a need within me that must be quenched. When the time comes, I become ill. Angry. Frustrated. I cannot be still. I do not sleep. The cravings are relentless, the addiction incurable. Not even Jean can stand to be near me."

"Andrea," Truman said, coming to her again.

"It will never be possible for you to hate what I am more than I do. I've wished a thousand times not to be this way. A million, perhaps." She shook her head. "So much do I hate the monster within me that I've learned to subdue the desires for long periods, but no, I cannot stop them completely."

"That's why, once a year…" Truman trailed off, unwilling to speak the words.

"I feed," she said, finishing his sentence.

"But why do you do….that to them?"

Andrea turned her head, ashamed. "When the beast comes, it is angry, tortured. Even after all these years, it is just a little girl who has been hurt, and it lashes out. For me, it is like watching a horrific movie, but I hear their screams. I watch them die."

Truman moved around her, lifting her chin.

She nodded as her eyes met his. "I feed on innocent people, and you bury the dead." A sad smile came to her lips. "At least you have freed poor Jean of his duties, and for that, he is thankful."

"So, Jean knows?"

"Of course, he knows." She crossed her arms on her chest, clinging to her elbows. "But there is something you should know about Jean."

Truman stiffened. "Is he your lover?"

Andrea shook her head. "No. He is not my lover. Jean is my son."

"Your son?" Truman asked, shocked.

Andrea nodded. "He is the result of a union of the Holy and the Unholy, though it is difficult to tell which was which."

"You mean…?"

Andrea nodded. "He is very human and so very old. I have done what I can for him, but he has informed me that this would be his last season. He loves this old hotel, and this is where he will perish."

"I'm sorry. I really like him."

"I know that, and so does he. Like I said before, you are a good man, Truman."

"What about you? What will you do?"

Andrea sighed. "Again, I must leave one place and find another. This isn't the first time, but I'm afraid it will be the most difficult."

"Because you're leaving Jean behind?" Truman asked.

"And you," she said, putting a hand along his cheek.

"I could go with you," Truman said, hope rising in his eyes.

Andrea smiled sadly, caressing his cheek with her thumb. "No. I have watched poor Jean all these years. He resents me in silence. I know he does. He should have been at rest so many years ago, but my selfishness keeps him with me." She dropped her hand from Truman's cheek and walked to the painting on the far wall, looking it over with a sad sigh. "I fear being alone, without you forever."

Truman looked at her, then at the painting on the wall next to her, his eyes finding the scant image of the woman in the bottom corner. The full weight of the darkness within the painting, the sadness, fell on him, and his heart sank. The woman in the painting had no more fashioned her own fate than Andrea had. Their fates had been thrust upon them to bear for eternity, one by an artist, the other by a monster masquerading as a priest. She could have gone her whole life without spilling a man's blood and would never have changed.

Truman crossed the room, embracing her from behind. She moaned quietly and nestled her head against him as he rested his chin on her shoulder.

"I have come to know two absolutes in all these years. The first is that this is my fate alone. I must bear this myself. It is who I am, not anyone else. Poor Jean has missed out on so much because of me. A wife. Children. A home. Happiness." Her hand came up and caressed Truman's cheek. "Love."

"There must be something we can do."

Andrea spun in his arms, her teary eyes finding his. "This is not a malady that can be fixed, Truman. It is who I am. It is what I am." She tore from his grasp and walked to the door. "I am a monster."

"You are not a monster," he insisted, joining her by the door. "Stop saying that. You're not."

"Will you say that when the sun comes up and you are called to do your duty?"

"Andrea, all I know is that I love you. I've never felt this way for anyone. Not even close. Everything else is just…"

"Can't you see? A life with me would be a prison for you, Truman. The years would pass, and it would slowly chip away at your soul like it has done Jean's. In time, you would come to resent me as well, maybe even hate me."

"No. Never."

"I see in your eyes something that wasn't there just a few hours ago when you were kissing my feet in the bath. The glimmer of your affection is still there, still strong, but it has already faded a little. In time, it would disappear completely, and I could not bear to see that."

Truman shook his head but said nothing. Despite the tragedy of her story, they were together. Now, it felt as if he were losing her all over again.

"We make love well together. So many nights, my body craved yours, but I restrained. I did not want to arrive at this very point, yet here we are. With you, as I have been with Jean, I was selfish. I believe that you think what you say is true, but you've only found out what I am, and already, your feelings have changed." She wiped a tear from her cheek.

"Nothing has changed," he said. "I'm just tired. It's been a long night."

Andrea smiled. "I wish that were true, but we both know that it isn't." She wiped another tear from her cheek with one hand and opened the door with the other. "I should go."

"I don't want you to go."

"Things have changed for us."

"Nothing has changed. Stay."

Andrea sighed. "Do you know what else I learned at a very young age, Truman? The other absolute?" Her eyes locked on his, narrowing slightly. "I learned that a man can fuck you and still despise everything that you are."

Truman stepped back from her, struck by her comment. The weight of it hit him like a hammer, and his chest suddenly felt heavy. He looked into her eyes and found only the cold truth that she had carried with her all these years.

After a moment, he saw her move to the door. So much of him wanted her to stay, to take her in his arms and hold her. There was also a part of him that knew she was right despite his refusal to admit it. Things were different.

When his name left her lips as she said goodbye, it came with a catch in her throat. He moved to her and saw the tears on her cheeks glimmering in the dim light. She bent forward and kissed his lips softly.

When she broke the kiss, he stared into her eyes, absorbing the agony within them. She wanted to stay as badly as he wanted her to, but she was stronger than he was. She'd long known the truth that he was just finding out and had time to prepare herself for it.

"Let me go," she whispered. "Please."

Truman stood motionless, frozen by everything his tired brain had heard. He watched her turn to leave, yet still couldn't move. He blinked tears from his eyes, blurring her image as she moved away from him and into the darkness. When he called her name, she hesitated for only a moment, but it was enough. His hands were around her wrist, gripping like a vice.

"Please," she begged, resisting his embrace.

"No." He pulled her into the room and slammed the door shut. Pushing her against it, he pressed his lips to hers, and they melted into a frantic kiss.

"Truman, please. I must go."

"No. Not now. Please. Not like this."

"Then how and when?" She cradled his face in her hands. "The sun will rise soon, and you will know."

"I don't care. Stay with me." He pulled her toward the bed. "Just lay with me. Let me hold you in my arms."

Andrea burst into tears as he tugged her across the room. "You do know that I love you?"

"I know. That's all that matters."

"For tonight."

"Yes, for tonight," he agreed. His hands found her shoulders and slipped the robe down as his lips worked their way down her neck.

"Tonight," she whispered, losing herself to his touch.

Truman pushed the robe over her shoulders and let it fall to the floor at their feet. Taking her hand, he brought her to his bed. Joining her, his lips found her lips, then her neck, then her shoulders. Andrea sank to the bed beneath him, gasping as his warm mouth found the nape of her neck.

"Truman," she moaned.

Saying nothing, his hands moved her fully onto her stomach. He moved above her, his lips finding the first scar. Beneath him, her body tensed, and her hands found the covers, clenching into fists. His kisses continued without hesitation as his mouth explored the length of the scar and moved to the next.

A violent shiver ran through her, and she closed her eyes, surrendering to him. A quiet moan escaped her and slipped into the shadows that enveloped them.

CHAPTER TWENTY-ONE

June 5th. Late morning

Truman awoke suddenly from a fitful sleep. Sweat plastered his hair to his head. His cheeks were sticky with dried tears. His first breath reminded him of the weight in his chest as his confused mind lurched to consciousness.

He opened his eyes in a panic but saw nothing but a dark room. Disoriented, his only thought was of Andrea. Where was she? Did she really leave? Would she come back? Hands frantically searched the bed next to him, finding nothing but empty sheets.

Turning, his heart thundering in his ears, hands flailing along his bedside table, knocking things over until he found the light. Switching it on, he looked around at the familiar setting that somehow now felt foreign. He was in his own room but had no memory of coming to it.

For an instant, he hoped that it had all been a dream, that last night had never happened, that Andrea wasn't gone. His heart swelled with hope but fell just as quickly as reality crashed down around him. It hadn't been a dream. Last night had happened. Both the good and the bad.

His stomach knotted. The light dropped to the floor as his hands went to his face. She couldn't be gone. Despite everything she'd told him, the thought of never seeing her again made his whole body ache. Even now, knowing that she was the one responsible for all the deaths, he still longed to be with her. He still loved her, but he hated himself for doing so. How could he still love her knowing the truth?

His head snatched up as the desire to run to her room swept through him like a current. He had to know. He had to prove that it was real, that she was gone. He sprung from the bed, finding a towel on the floor next to the light. It was the towel Andrea had worn around her head.

He grabbed it, bringing it to his face. It still smelled of the soft fragrance of her hair. Closing his eyes, he held the towel to his face, and she was with him again. She wasn't gone. She'd just gone to help her father with something.

He held the towel before him in a fist as his other hand pushed through his hair. No. Andrea wasn't helping Jean. She was gone.

Crossing the room, he wrapped the towel around himself. He had to know. He needed to see her room. If she wasn't there. He'd check the kitchen and the lounge. The utility rooms. The roof. He'd searched every inch of the hotel before he believed she was gone.

Energized by hope, he snatched the door open, and his whole world came to a screeching halt. Suddenly, his body was too heavy to stand. His chest felt as if he'd taken a punch. Hands pushed over his face and then through his hair, interlacing his fingers behind his head. He gasped for air as he stared at the painting, leaning against the wall opposite his door. Andrea's painting. The one with the forlorn woman.

But it was more than a painting. It was confirmation, a truth he didn't want to face. She was everything that she said she was, and she was gone. There was no denying it now. Staggering forward, he half knelt, half-collapsed to his knees.

Trembling hands lifted the painting, and a note dropped to the floor. He grabbed it up and retreated into his room. Fresh tears began to flow as he carried the painting to the bed. Grabbing the lamp, he sat it on the table, illuminating the painting now across his lap. His fingers went to the woman in the painting, gently caressing her image as his tears littered the canvas.

Balancing the painting on his knees, he wiped his face with the back of his hand and then opened the note.

> *Truman,*
> *I will always love you, for you are the only person*
> *who has brought me true happiness other than my son,*
> *yet I have caused you both great pain. For this*
> *I am truly sorry. Remember me, please, with love.*
> *For I shall love thee with a love that shall not die*
> *till the sun grows cold and the stars grow old.*
> *Forever, Andrea*

His fingertips went to her gentle flowing script, wishing to hold the hand that had written it. His eyes found a small, discolored spot near the bottom of the note. Andrea's tear had fallen to the page as she told him goodbye. His thumb found the stain and caressed it. He imagined her sitting in her room crying, not wanting to leave, and his breath caught in his throat.

The desire to go to her room was gone. She wasn't there. He knew that now. She was gone, and he'd never see her again.

Rising from the bed, he carried the painting across the room. Putting it down gently, he removed the framed print of a Monet that had hung in the room since he'd moved in. The field of colorful wildflowers no longer suited him. Retrieving Andrea's painting, he hung it on the wall in its place.

Staring at the painting, his vision drifting in and out with the tears flowing from his eyes, his fingertips found the forlorn lady, and his heart sank further.

His heart ached not only for himself and what he'd lost but for Andrea as well. Wherever she was, her heart was broken too, worse than his, for she was truly alone.

Closing his eyes, he thought again of the first time he saw her, and a sad smile tugged at the corners of his mouth. His shoulders slumped, and his fingers slipped from the painting, barely catching on the frame.

He opened his eyes to his splayed fingertips, for the first time seeing the artist's initials barely peeping from behind the frame. He hurried to the table and returned with the lamp, holding it against the painting.

His eyes flew wide, and his heart stopped in his chest. In the bottom right corner, he found two capital A's painted in dark maroon, hidden in the darkness of the shadows. A.A. Andrea Ardelean.

He stared at the painting, letting his tears flow freely as his appreciation for it grew. She'd left him a piece of herself, a look inside her own pain. Her words echoed in his mind.

I fear being alone, without you forever.

His fingertip brushed ever so slightly across the initials, and he gasped, suddenly remembering the other paintings in her room.

Clad in only a towel, Truman burst into Andrea's room. His eyes went to her bed, hoping that she'd be there, though he knew she wouldn't. It was undisturbed, perfectly made, as usual.

Turning, he went to the first painting, thrusting the light against it. His eyes tried to focus in the dim light, but the batteries were fading fast. Looking around the room, his eyes were drawn to the scant light sneaking in around the plywood that had never been attached to her windows.

He went to the closest one and wrestled it from behind the heavy drapes. The soft glow of the day flooded the room. He went back to the painting but still couldn't be sure of the signature. Cursing the fading lamp, he snatched the painting from the wall and took it to the window. Holding the painting in the light, he moved it back and forth until the light hit it just right. His eyes went to the bottom right corner and found the same initials. A.A.

Buoyed by his find, he retrieved another picture, finding the same initials. Moving quickly, he repeated the process with the fourth painting in the set. Removing it from the wall, he stared at the initials with a mixture of joy and overwhelming sadness.

Overcome, he dropped into the padded wingback chair, clutching the last painting. Staring at the crescent moon, a smile tried to blossom on his lips. Having the paintings wasn't as good as having her, but at least he had enough of her to draw consolation from. She'd poured her heart into each of the paintings, and now they were his, forever, just like his memories of her. They were all that was left of her now.

"She was a masterful painter, but I always found her subject matter heartbreaking."

Truman looked up to find Jean standing in the open door, a letter clutched in his hand. His face was drawn with an anguish that matched his own. Truman nodded, then looked at the painting on his lap.

"She said that she had to paint the way she felt."

Truman's fingers found the woman in the painting before him. The sorrow in the work was almost palpable.

"She is a tortured soul, my friend," Jean said as he crossed the room and sat down on Andrea's bed. Leaning forward, he rested his elbows on his knees. His head dropped with a shuttered sigh. "But I love her still."

"Will she ever come back?" Truman asked quietly.

Jean shrugged. "I do not know. Sometimes, I do not understand the things she does."

"Yes, you do," Truman said.

Jean nodded slightly, his head still hung low. "What did she tell you?"

"Everything." Truman closed his eyes, sighing. "Well, enough, I guess. I know about her."

"It's not her fault, you know."

"I know. She told me her story. Or at least the beginning." Truman wiped his eyes with the heel of his hand. "I just don't understand any of it. It all seems so…" he shook his head, unable to come up with a fitting word to describe the situation.

"She always hated what she became, but this life was put upon her, Truman. She did not choose it, nor could she change it. She was a prisoner in so many ways."

"What about you?"

Jean shrugged. "I guess you could say the same thing for me."

Truman stared at Jean as he wept quietly. "Are you like her?"

Jean shook his head. "No. I am not completely as you are, but neither am I like her. But I have been with her for a great many years. I am very old. Much older than I was ever meant to be."

Truman watched Jean waver, then steady himself. "Are you going to be okay?"

Jean nodded. "I am as well as I can be. I can already feel her absence in my bones."

"How long have you both been here? The whole time?"

Jean smiled as he shook his head. "We came to this area a very long time ago. Because it was secluded and unchecked, she chose it to…" he trailed off, waving a hand in the air. "You know."

Truman nodded, glad that Jean hadn't used the word "feed."

"We moved around a lot. Every ten years or so. That

seemed to be how long it took for people to notice that her looks didn't change much. People would get curious, then we would leave." He raised his head, staring at the wall.

"We fled the old country because there were men who hunted people like her. There once were many, but now there are few. Some enjoyed the life. Many did not. We traveled, and then she found this region. It is a beautiful country. When we first came, she told everyone that I was her son. As the years passed, we pretended that I was her brother. Then, her husband. More years passed, and I became her father. Every new town, there was a new story."

"You do know that I love her?"

Jean nodded. "I have always known." He tossed his letter on the bed and pushed a hand through his hair. "You must know that she had to leave."

"Why?"

"Already there is talk. People accepted the sequester well enough, but they still talked about Andrea. We've been in this town for over a dozen years now. She is very beautiful. People notice things. Especially beautiful women."

"Still," Truman persisted.

"It's not that simple. It always begins with whispers, then talk. Men would come and try to kill her, eventually."

"She could defend herself."

Jean nodded in agreement. "To what end? More men would come, then more, then more. It would never end. She did not enjoy what she had to do, Truman. In the beginning, she resisted the urges as long as she could. Then, as she came to control them better, she hunted in the spring. As time passed, people began to see a pattern, so they hid on certain days. Ultimately, she was able to resist most of the time, limiting her need."

Truman cast his eyes to the painting again, wondering how much pain Andrea had endured in her lifetime. "That's how the sequester started?"

"Yes. That made it easier for her." He gave a weak shrug.

Truman rubbed his forehead and then drug his hand down his face. That explained the seemingly random date.

Jean sighed heavily. "Another reason that she left was that she also had to leave me."

"What does that mean?"

"She has been the force that has kept me alive this long. Forgive me, please, but I am very old and so tired. My body needs to find rest."

Truman looked up at Jean, and he nodded. Though he didn't think it possible, his heart fell further. Not only did he lose Andrea, but he'd lose Jean as well.

"How long?"

"It's hard to say. It could be weeks, but not more than a few months."

Truman drew in a deep breath and let it out slowly. "Will she ever find peace?"

"That I do not know." Jean pushed himself up from the bed with a groan. "I hope she does. I know that she's caused her share of suffering by doing what she had to do, but she's borne a tremendous amount of shame and guilt as well."

Truman watched Jean make his way to the door. "She was a good mother to me when I was young and a good companion when I grew old. I will miss her dearly for as long as I live."

Truman nodded. "Me too."

A sad smile comes to Jean's lips. "If it's any consolation, I believe that you were the only man she's ever truly loved. You made her very happy, and I cannot thank you enough for that."

"A lot of good it did."

Jean shook his head. "The slightest flame, no matter how fleeting, can warm the right heart in the darkest of nights. And so can its memory."

CHAPTER TWENTY-TWO

December 23rd. Late Evening

Decked out with crystal ornaments, green and purple balls, and gold ribbons, Truman thought the Christmas tree before him was probably the gaudiest he'd ever seen, but it somehow fit perfectly in the lobby of the Jupiter Hotel.

The staff had done their best to replicate the design that Andrea had always followed, but it didn't look the same. Then again, the whole place had lost some of its charm since she'd gone.

He might have been tempted to leave, to find somewhere else to live, but Jean's health had gotten worse, and he needed a friend to look after him. Aside from Andrea, Truman was the only person he trusted.

The fact that Jean had turned the hotel over to him was another reason he stayed. He quickly found out that the pension of a small-town police officer wasn't a lot, and the extra income and lack of a rent payment helped more than he cared to admit.

But the real reason he stayed was Andrea. There were too many good memories of her here. Every day, he'd see something, and a memory of her would surface. Simple things like the straw in a drink or a sandwich. Dust on the chandelier. There was still so much of her here that it was easy to pretend. Some days, he allowed himself to believe that she was just busy. Those days were better than most, and he was able to concentrate on the hotel, which now seemed to need constant repair.

Then night would come, and he'd trudge up the stairs to his room. He would sit alone and look at her paintings and remember the times they shared. He would lay in bed and wonder where she was and what she was doing. He often wondered if she was still as sad as he was.

He hadn't rented out her room, leaving it just as it had been the last time she was in it. He visited it often, even after her scent had left the sheets, just to get a better sense of her presence.

Sometimes, late at night, he'd sit in her chair and read a few pages of her books. When he came across one not written in English, he'd just sit and imagine her eyes as they moved back and forth across the passages.

Of course, his friends worried about him. When one of them came by, he'd put on a smile and tell them he was okay. He knew that he wasn't, and they probably did, too, but that was fine. He'd probably never be okay again, but he was getting better. Time had taken the razor's edge off his pain, allowing him to enjoy moments like this and to see the situation more clearly. Most of the anger he felt because she'd left had withered. She was in an impossible situation and had done an amazing job mitigating the effects on everyone around her.

She'd never asked for the life she had. It was forced upon her. In so many ways, she was as helpless as he was. Through the long nights filled with tears and loneliness, two truths had worked their way to the surface. The first was that she was no monster. Not even close.

Jean had explained to him the pain she suffered by not feeding regularly. Her joints would ache, and her muscles cramped. The thought of feeding would build until it became an obsession, consuming her with rage and an animalistic hunger.

He likened it to a heroin junkie going through withdrawals, all while having as much junk at his disposal as he could stand.

The fact that she could go through that and still function amazed him. The amount of sheer willpower that she must have possessed was beyond his comprehension and made him appreciate her more.

The other truth that surfaced was the fact that he still loved her. Through his anger, his resentment, and his cursing of the situation, that was the one thing that remained constant. He said the words to her every night as he drifted off to sleep, and he meant it every time.

———

Truman sighed, forcing a smile as he looked at the tree. "We did our best. Please forgive us." Shaking his head, he turned and slowly climbed his way up the stairs, pausing only a moment to look at Andrea's paintings.

The art lights shone down on each one, chasing away the shadows and giving the moon depicted in each painting a soft glow. Someone had suggested he have them appraised, but he never would. To him, they were priceless. They were painted by Andrea's delicate hand, and he'd never part with any of them.

He wanted them here so he could see them throughout the day. Whenever he passed, he could look up and catch sight of a piece of her. Some of the guests didn't appreciate the darkness depicted in them, but he'd always remind them that there couldn't be light without darkness.

Moving around the mule post, he climbed the steps to the third-floor as he'd done countless times, but instead of turning left to go to his room, he turned right.

He paused at Jean's door and looked at the door to Andrea's room. He closed his eyes, hoping that she would step through the door. When he opened them, and she wasn't there, he sighed.

Turning to the door next to him, he knocked softly. "Jean?" he called as he opened it slowly. "It's Truman."

Jean was lying down with his eyes closed, the light of the television at the foot of his bed chasing away the shadows. Truman's shoulders slumped. He didn't mind looking after the old man, he figured he owed him that much, but this was his least favorite task.

Jean went downhill quickly in Andrea's absence, as he predicted he would. Aging badly, he was relegated mostly to the third floor within weeks. He'd been bedridden for a month now. They both knew the end was close.

Truman crept to the bed and picked up the remote, switching off the television. The lamp next to the bed cast a pale light onto his face. The lines of old age were relaxed, and the furrow in his brow that had come with the pain was now gone.

Truman sighed. Stepping closer, he laid two fingers against the side of Jean's neck. When he felt no pulse, he pressed harder. Still, there was nothing. He lifted Jean's hand and checked the pulse on his wrist. Nothing.

Truman stepped back and sat down hard in a chair next to the bed. He'd brought Jean's dinner up just hours ago. He didn't eat much, but that was becoming typical, so he didn't worry. He could ask housekeeping how he was when they collected the tray, but it didn't matter.

"Well, old friend, you're finally at rest." Truman thumbed a tear from the corner of his eye. "I'm just sorry you had to die alone."

"He didn't die alone."

Truman spun in the chair as a figure stepped out of the shadows of the darkened bathroom. His heart stopped at the sound of her voice.

Rising unsteadily from the chair, he watched, frozen by an avalanche of emotions, as she stepped into the light. He wanted to run to her, to embrace her, but he didn't.

Was she just here for Jean or for him? He'd fought tooth and nail to survive losing her already. He couldn't do it again. Reopening his heart only to have her leave again would finish him.

"Do you hate me?" she asked softly. When Truman didn't answer, she added, "Because you have every right to."

Finally, he sighed and shook his head. "No," he whispered as a tear rolled down his cheek. "I never hated you."

She moved closer, extending a hand toward him. "May I?"

Truman remained still, but her hand touched his face and collected the tear from his cheek.

"I am truly sorry for the pain I have caused you."

Truman's eyes washed over her. She was as beautiful as ever. Dressed in a long black dress, with her hair resting on one shoulder, she looked as if time hadn't passed at all. The months might have been seconds.

His eyes found hers, and a smile parted her lips, weakening his resolve. "I still love you."

"I know," she said, caressing his cheek. "I spoke with Jean for a long time before he passed. He was upset with me." She looked at the bed, and a tear spilled from her eye. "But only because I hurt you."

"We've grown quite close lately."

She looked back at Truman. "Did he tell you that he would not have ever passed if I had stayed?"

"He explained everything about you."

Andrea nodded, her hand falling from Truman's cheek. "He knows every detail, the poor soul."

"Well, he's at rest now."

She nodded again, a tear escaping the corner of her eye. She collected it quickly. "But you are not."

"I'll make do," Truman lied. His knees were getting weak,

and it was becoming hard to breathe.

"Will you?"

Truman shrugged. "Do I have a choice, Andrea?"

Andrea's eyes shifted back to Jean, and she sighed. "Did he?"

"He loved you too."

"Still…"

"He always had a choice. Don't you see that? When he was done, he told you."

"It was unfair to him."

"You don't get it, do you?"

"I understand perfectly," she said, turning from him.

"I don't think you understand at all." Truman went to her and grabbed her arm. When she spun to him with fire in her eyes, he held her gaze.

"I can only bring people pain."

"Jean loved you. That's why he stayed with you. He could have left you years ago, but he didn't. He loved you and wanted to be with you."

"And look at him!" she snapped, snatching her arm free of his grasp.

"You know something, Jean and I talked a lot. He told me stories about his life. The places he went, the things he saw. His eyes twinkled when he told those stories. They were full of adventure and friends. He didn't look like a man forced into anything. He looked like a man who had a full, rich life and enjoyed all of it."

Andrea looked at Jean, and another tear ran down her cheek. "He was a loyal companion to the end."

"He chose his own life, the life he wanted."

"Well, I didn't," she said, turning back to Truman.

"That's the problem, Andrea. You couldn't imagine anyone could love you because of what happened to you. You hate this fragment of who you are and fail to see the real you. You see yourself as only a monster, just like they told you were when you were a little girl."

"I'm not a scared little girl anymore."

Truman sighed as he searched her eyes. "Aren't you, though?" He watched anger rise in her eyes, then fade slowly, replaced by regret.

"I should have never revealed myself to you," she said, shaking her head.

"Then why did you bother? You knew you were going to leave. Just like now. You're just going to leave again, aren't you? This time, though, you won't have a reason to ever come back."

Andrea's eyes fell, and he had his answer.

"I'm not going to beg you to stay this time. I can't."

Andrea pursed her lips and turned from him, wiping tears from her face. "Your feelings for me have cooled, I see. Have you found another woman?"

Truman grunted in disbelief. "The problem is that you see yourself as a monster, and you can't fathom why someone would want to be with you. What you refuse to see is that someone can actually love you. That someone is willing to look beyond what you see in yourself and love the person that is you."

Truman shrugged, tossing his hands into the air when she didn't respond. "Jean loved you. Yes, he knew every detail about you, but he still loved you enough to devote his life to you. Just like I was willing to do."

"Was?" she asked.

"I don't want to watch you hate yourself, Andrea. I love you too much to go through that." Truman walked to the door. "You carry so much anger over what happened to you, and rightfully so. I can't say I blame you. It's the self-loathing I can't stand. I know now that's why you were so violent when you released that part of yourself. You took your anger out on everyone around you in one way or another."

Truman went to the door and opened it. "I'm sorry, Andrea. If you're going to go, then just go. I need to make arrangements for Jean."

Truman stepped out the door and pulled it closed behind him. In the hall, he staggered and fell against the wall. His hands went to his face to cover the tears he couldn't stop from coming. His mind was in chaos. His heart hung like a lead weight in his chest.

He staggered down the hallway, each step a struggle until he finally made it to his room. He opened the door and stepped inside.

"You have no right to say that."

Truman stopped suddenly, falling back against the door as it closed. He dug his fists into his bleary eyes and shook his head. When he looked up, Andrea was standing in the center of his room.

"What the…how?"

"Never mind that," Andrea said, coming to him as he staggered to a chair and sat down hard. "You said you love me, yet you speak to me in such a way."

"I do love you." Truman pushed a hand through his hair. "I've had a lot of nights to examine our affair, my feelings. It wasn't just lust. It was so much more than that. Your simple presence in my life, no matter how minor, brought me joy. Your presence in this hotel changed the whole feel of this place. I didn't even have to see you, but just knowing you were here made me feel better. I told you that. Your leaving was like winter coming to a garden. All the beauty was gone, all the life."

Truman stood and looked at her. "I do still love you. That's why I'm telling you the truth."

"You don't know what truth is."

"Don't I?"

"No. You don't," she snapped.

"I know the truth about you, Andrea. You see, people like me and Jean, people who really love you, we see you. The real you."

"The real me?" Her jaw clenched as she stared at him. "This is the real me!" She threw her hands out, allowing herself to change, assuming the form she took while hunting.

Truman shrank in horror, watching as she grew taller, nearly reaching the ten-foot ceiling. The beautiful face he loved to look at took on a hideously savage complexion with a heavy brow and dull skin thin enough to allow every coursing blood vessel to show through.

The sparkling eyes that enamored him were now deep-set orbs, dark and angry as they stared down at him. Her thick crop of delicate hair faded into thin, wispy clumps, hanging limply about the pallid skin of her head.

Towering over him, her clothes now in tatters, her long arms closed in around him. Truman grimaced as the sharp claws at the end of her hands gripped his shoulders.

Leaning forward, she brought her face close to his as a gaping mouth opened. Thick strands of saliva stretched between rows of sharp, pointed teeth. When her mouth was fully agape, two long incisors slid down from the roof of her mouth. She drew in a deep breath and, bending close to him, screamed into his face. The sound was somewhere between a shriek of pain and terror and the angry roar of a large animal.

When she finished her scream, she stood seething at him, her hot breath washing over his face in waves. Truman shook his head. It was easy to see how she'd done such damage to the houses and her victims. He stared at her in shock. His heart was racing, but he felt no fear. She wouldn't hurt him, and he knew it.

"No," he finally said. "This isn't the real you."

Andrea's body shuttered as she quickly morphed back to

the form he was used to seeing. She released his shoulders, and her knees buckled. She tumbled to the floor, sobbing.

The dress that had fit her so well now barely clung to her, a torn mess. The strap over her right shoulder had broken, allowing the fabric to droop far enough to reveal the first scars on her back.

Truman went to her immediately, kneeling behind her. Reaching around her, he took her trembling hands in his and held her. When she resisted, he tightened his grip.

"While, admittedly, that was a little scary, it doesn't change anything."

Andrea grunted and raised a hand to pull the dress up on her back. She wanted to hide her scars, but he stopped her. Leaning forward, he put his lips on the scar at the nape of her neck and kissed it.

"Actually," he whispered, "It's not as bad as I'd imagined in my head."

"You are a damned fool," she said, a weak chuckle forcing its way through her sobs.

"Probably. But what man in love isn't?"

She spun in his arms. Her eyes frantically searched his face as a hand rose to his cheek. "How could you possibly love me after seeing that?"

"Because that's not who you are."

"But it is," she insisted. "Don't you see that? You cannot pretend that it isn't. I cannot pretend."

"That's what other people made you, Andrea. That's what they did to you. It's not the real you. You are the woman who gets pleasure from helping people who take care of people. You're the woman who takes the time to wrap sandwiches with perfect folds and smiley-faced stickers because you care about strangers and want to bring them some joy, even if they don't know it."

Truman pushed a hand through her hair, watching it slide

between his fingers. "You are beautiful and kind, passionate. You are caring and attentive. You genuinely enjoy making people happy. That's who you are. That's the woman I love."

"But I am also the other."

"Yes. I know."

"And you couldn't love that part of me." Her eyes dropped as more tears began to flow again.

"You don't know that. I might have a kink. It was pretty tall. You know, I kinda dig tall chicks."

Andrea looked up at him, perturbed. "This is not a time for your silly jokes, Truman."

"I don't know. A wig, a little make-up. Go easy on the claws. It might be a fun change of pace every now and then."

"Stop it," she said as she squirmed in his arms, trying to get away. When he refused to let her go, she gave up and relaxed. "It was supposed to scare you enough to make my leaving easier."

Truman shrugged. "What can I say? I was raised in an era when they made movies with the intent to give kids nightmares."

"You were not frightened only because you knew I'd never hurt you," she said, laying her head on his chest.

"While that is true, I might have peed a little bit at first."

A chuckle escaped her. "Some days I wish you didn't love me."

"And others?" he asked.

"That's the only thing that keeps me alive."

"I know you love me, Andrea."

She wrapped her arms around him, clinging to him tightly. "I do so love you. I've loved you so hard for so long."

"Then let me love you back."

"It is not that simple."

"Yes, it is. I've loved you for years already."

"And what of me? I get to watch you grow old, become sick, die a slow death like Jean?" She shook her head. "That would hurt me more than leaving you now." She tried to pull away again, but he held her.

"Let me go, Truman."

"I can't do that."

"Please."

"Not a chance."

Andrea gave one final effort to free herself, then gave up with a sigh.

"There is another way."

She looked at him, shocked. "No," she said.

"Why not?"

"This is not a life you want, Truman."

"The only life I want is with you. Everything else is window dressing."

"You don't know what you are saying. This—" she swept a hand down her body— "is not window dressing, Truman. It is very real and very unpleasant at times."

"What? I can't go in the sun?" Truman shrugged. "I'm more of a mountain person than a beach person anyway."

Andrea rolled her eyes. "You infuriate me with your stupid jokes."

"I've told you, it's a character flaw. You have your thing and I tell jokes at inopportune times. See, we all have our flaws."

"This is not a joke, Truman. You are a fool for even thinking it."

"I think we've established that I'm a fool. Look, I don't care what it entails. I want to be with you. That's all that matters. Right now, I only have two choices. A life with you and all that goes with it, or a lonely, miserable existence for the next thirty years or until I simply wither and die. That's it. There's you or nothing."

"There are other women, Truman. Stop being such a f—" She almost called him a fool again but caught herself. "I can't do this to you. Find a good woman and live the rest of your life in peace. Grow old together and find happiness together."

"But there's no other Andrea Ardelean. Every moment, I'd be comparing her to you, and she'd fall short. I'd hate her because she wasn't you, and she'd hate me for loving another woman."

Truman moved in front of her, taking her face in his hands. "I've never ached for something, for someone like I've ached for you these past few months. I'm ashamed to admit it, but if I wasn't such a coward, I'd probably have shoved a gun in my mouth and pulled the trigger."

"Truman, no."

"It's true," he said with a shrug. "I spent weeks in bed, drinking myself into oblivion. Jean made the bar stop serving me, so I bought my own. I couldn't face a world without you in it. I sat in your room and read your books. Or at least tried to. I said goodnight to you every night."

She searched his eyes, looking for the truth. "This life is not one I would have chosen for myself, Truman. It is one of remorse, of guilt."

"I don't care, Andrea. A life without you will be one of remorse and loneliness."

She nodded. "I know loneliness."

"Then you know what I mean. There will be no one else for me. It is you or no one."

"I can't."

"Can you tell me that, wherever you were, you haven't thought about me? Wanted to be with me?"

"I have. My soul ached for you. I started a hundred times to come back just to watch you sleep."

"Then why didn't you?"

"Because I knew this would happen. I knew I would want to stay with you. I knew if I saw you, I'd never want to leave."

"Is that such a bad thing?"

She nodded. "With me, it is."

"Don't do this to me again. Please. It's my choice. If this is what it takes, then it's what I want."

"Truman, you must be sure. There will be no going back."

"I know. But there will be you."

"You will have to feed. On innocent people. Truman, they will die. You're a good man, and that is not something I could ask you to do."

"Don't you think I've thought about that? In the weeks after you left, I told myself I could do it without remorse if only I had you."

"And after that?" she asked, her eyes searching his.

"If the choices were to never be with you and be miserable or to feed on innocent people and feel regret, I'd choose you."

A sad smile came to her lips. "It would be a difficult transition for you."

"Probably so."

"It is hard on your body. The first day will decide if you live or die."

Truman shrugged. "Is death worse than a lifetime of loneliness?"

Andrea shook her head. "We would have to leave here, never stay anywhere for more than a few years."

"Okay. I hear Paris is nice this time of year."

Andrea shook her head. "Winters in Paris are long and cold and wet."

"Oh, I meant Paris, Texas," he said with a grin.

She closed her eyes and sighed, pushing through his attempt at levity. "Truman," her eyes dropped from his. "I will not bear children for you. It would be unfair to them."

"Look, I'm fifty years old," he said, lifting her chin. "That's not a problem." He bent and kissed her lips. "So, are you going to bite me or what?"

"You are a fool."

"You're the one who is about to commit to an eternity of my bad jokes."

"Hmm," he said with a smile. "I hadn't considered that."

Truman kissed her again. "Andrea Ardelean, I'll love you until the sun grows cold," he said.

"And the stars grow old," she added.

Truman pulled her to him and kissed her lips.

CHAPTER TWENTY-THREE

"So," Truman said with a grin. "Are we going to do this or not?"

Andrea rolled her eyes as she pushed her tattered dress down her body. Turning her back to Truman, she kicked it into the corner.

Truman's eyes fell on her scarred back, and a shutter ran through him. How much had the beating hurt, especially for a child? More than he could have withstood.

Andrea pulled on one of Truman's tee shirts and turned to him. "You say this as if we were ordering wine or picking out a pet."

"Oh no. Picking out a pet is hard."

"Truman," she said, her face drawn into a serious look.

"I'm sorry. No more jokes, but if there's a chance this will kill me, do you think we could…" he jerked his head toward the bed behind him, wiggling his eyebrows.

She looked at him, unamused. "This is serious, Truman."

She joined him as he sat on the edge of the bed and put a hand along his cheek. Staring into his eyes, she added, "The fact that you'd consider it makes my heart full, but I cannot let you do it."

"It's not your choice."

She nodded. "It is solely my choice, and I wouldn't want to curse you with the life that I have had."

Truman took her hand in his. "That's just it. I wouldn't have the life you did. This is America, not central Europe or wherever you were born."

Andrea shook her head, a thin smile coming to her lips. "Do you really think that there is more room for a monster like me in this world than there was in that one? Do you think they wouldn't do the same thing to me? Or worse?"

Truman sighed. She was right. There were many people in town, himself included, that would have killed her if they could have figured out a way.

"Still." He pushed a lock of hair back from her face and stared into her eyes. "If I have to live without you…"

"Truman, please."

"I want you. You. Whatever form or way it manifests, that's what I want."

"You will have to feed. On innocent people."

Truman nodded solemnly. "I know."

"It isn't a pleasant thing. You can't help yourself, but you remember all of it. The screams, the fear." She dropped her eyes to their hands. "The pain."

"Is there any other way?"

She looked up, fixing her eyes on his. "No."

"Then there's your answer."

Andrea pushed the hair back from Truman's forehead and smiled. "Are you sure?"

He nodded. "I am."

Opening her mouth, she revealed her fangs. Tilting her head to the side, she bent forward.

Truman's body tensed as her hot breath fell on his neck. Her mouth felt natural on his skin, welcomed. His eyes flew open as her teeth pierced his skin. The pain wasn't as bad as he expected, like two simultaneous pen pricks. Then the heat came.

The burning spread quickly along his neck, down to his

shoulder, with the most intense heat coming between the teeth. He groaned and stiffened. Her hands morphed into the hands she used while hunting, gripping him tighter. The tips of her fingernails pushed through his shirt and dug into his skin. Patches of crimson bloomed on his shirt around the tip of each claw.

When she finally pulled away, he saw blood on her lips. His blood. His head began to swim like he was drunk. Her voice came to him from miles away. He was falling back, his eyes trained on her. Strong hands helped him to the floor.

The ceiling of his room swam in and out of his vision. Then she was there, over him, her face draped in fear. Her voice grew more distant. Darkness closed in around his line of sight. He tried to raise his hand, but it wouldn't move.

His breaths were coming in short, rapid pants. His heart thundered in his chest. Sweat collected on his temple and ran into his hairline. Andrea's face was closer now, inches from his, as the darkness shrank his vision. She clung to him. Her bloodied lips moved in silence.

Truman closed his eyes once, felt her hand on his cheek, and opened them again. The look in her eyes was frantic. She was shaking him, but he couldn't respond.

A brief smile touched his lips, and then he closed his eyes again. A weight landed on his chest, but he'd drifted too far away to move.

"No, no, no. Truman." Andrea cradled his head in her hands, gently caressing his cheek. "Please, no." Tears poured from her eyes as she shook the limp body in front of her.

The scent of blood filled her nostrils. The taste of it was in her mouth, on the air. Her eyes widened, pupils dilated, as primal urges tried to come forward. Struggling against her own body and hundreds of years of instincts, she pushed herself away from him.

Turning from Truman, her body wracked by the internal

struggle, she threw herself on the floor. Long talons dug into the floor, leaving deep gauges in the wood as she crawled away from him. She couldn't feed on Truman. She wouldn't.

A deep, animalistic growl escaped her as she fought the desire to feed. This was always the hardest part. Stopping. She craved blood like a junkie. On several occasions, Jean had to chain her to prevent her from continuing. She could have devoured the whole town before sating her appetite, but she didn't.

Clutching her transformed hand to her chest, she half crawled, half drug herself to the bathroom. Once inside, she closed the door, lessening the smell of Truman's blood. The cold tile felt good against the inferno raging inside her body, but she knew it wouldn't be enough.

A clawed hand reached up and grabbed the sink, talons digging gouges in the porcelain bowl. She pulled herself up onto unsteady legs. Turning on the cold water, she plunged her face into the stream.

Rivulets of Truman's blood washed from her mouth and circled the drain. She closed her eyes, not wanting to see the evidence of what she'd done. The one man who might have loved her was destroyed by the part of her that she hated the most. What a fool shed been to have even the slimmest of hope for happiness.

She rose slightly, using her human hand to splash water on her face. The urges faded some, but not enough. Dragging her wet hair out of her face as she stood, she stared into the mirror over the sink, seeing only the wall behind her.

Grimacing, she turned away, glad that she'd never been able to see herself. As if Truman's body wasn't enough, this was just one more reminder of the monster she really was.

Normally, Jean would be here to fill the tub with ice water. He would nurse her through the next few hours and care for her. But he was gone now. Everyone she'd ever cared about was gone.

First Jean, now Truman. For the first time in a very long time, she was alone. Completely, utterly alone.

The truth staggered her beneath its weight. She fell back against the wall and covered her face with her hands. The one that had changed was mostly back to normal now, but in her weakened state, she knew she wouldn't be able to contain it.

She needed to get away. She needed to go far away and rage. She needed to destroy and kill until her pain was spent. Now, there was no reason to fight it. Now, she could surrender to the beast within and let it free. There was no one left to pretend for.

Clenching her fists, she pounded them against the door. The sound of splintering wood and her low, guttural growl filled the bathroom, echoing back at her from the tile. Someone would surely hear, but she didn't care. It didn't matter anymore. Nothing did.

The wooden door gave way completely on her second strike, falling to the floor in the bedroom in ragged chunks. Her hands ripped frantically at the remaining wood, ripping it from the frame and tossing it aside.

She stormed into the bedroom that she'd visited more times than she could count. The scent of Truman Malone filled her nose, and so did the smell of his blood.

Her fists still clenched at her side, she closed her eyes and made herself smell him. She found the light, airy scent of his aftershave, the musky scent of his body. She smelled his skin when they kissed, the powerful aroma of his arousal when they made love. All of these she locked in her mind, never wanting to forget them. He was the only man besides Jean who ever knew her secret, who ever loved the real her, and she wanted to remember him forever.

Drawing in a hitchy breath, she sank to her knees as her pain came forth in tears. Falling forward, she let herself sob. They came in long, powerful waves that shook her body violently, but she didn't try to fight them. She couldn't have if she'd tried.

As Andrea drifted toward consciousness, her body began to register complaints about her sleeping arrangements. Her back and hips ached from sleeping on the hardwood floor. Her head pounded, and her face felt like a dried, crusted mask. Her parched throat felt cracked and burned.

A knock at the door snatched her up from the floor. She grimaced as her neck exploded in pain. Weak arms pushed her body into a sitting position. She'd been careless and succumbed to her emotional exhaustion. She should be miles from here by now, safely away from prying eyes. With Jean, she knew she'd have time, but Truman was another story. He'd be missed.

A female voice with a slight Spanish accent came through the door. "Mister Malone?" Andrea shook her head, admonishing herself again. "Are you okay, Mister Malone?"

Andrea did her best to impersonate Truman's voice despite the rawness of her throat. "I'm fine."

"It's just that when you didn't come down for breakfast or lunch, I started to get worried. When you didn't come for supper, I wanted to check on you."

Andrea cleared her throat. "I'm fine. Just tired."

"Are you sick? You don't sound well."

"I'm fine. Please, just leave." Andrea held her breath as she stared at the door, unsure if she'd fooled the woman or aroused more suspicion. "I have the flu," she said, adding a cough for emphasis.

"Okay. Should I call the doctor?"

"No."

"It's no bother."

"Please leave." Andrea pushed her hands through her wild tangle of hair, begging for the woman to go away. If she didn't, or if she decided to come in, things would escalate quickly.

"Okay. Feel better soon. Call if you need the doctor. But don't wait too long. It's best to catch these things early."

It wasn't until she heard footsteps walking away from the door that Andrea relaxed. Her eyes went immediately to the window. It was still dark outside, but she must have been sleeping for a long time. The woman had mentioned three meals. Had she been asleep for twenty-four hours?

"I don't sound like that."

Andrea spun at the voice, finding Truman slumped in the corner. Vomit had dried on the front of his shirt and on the floor around him. His skin was pale and his eyes weak, but the sight of him made her heart leap.

"Truman," she gasped, rushing to him. She sank to her knees beside him, ignoring the mess on the floor. Her hands cradled his face. "I thought you were gone."

He nodded weakly. "Me too."

She pushed his hair back from his face and smiled. "How do you feel?"

"Bad."

She clutched him to her chest. "I know. I'm so sorry." She pulled back, still holding him. "It will pass." Wiping his face, she leaned in and kissed his lips.

"You must really love me," he said. "Because my breath has got to be pretty bad right now."

Andrea's smile widened. "I do love you."

Truman closed his eyes, gathering his strength, but continued to smile. "Good. Because now you're stuck with me forever."

Andrea moved to lie against him. Wrapping her arms around his waist, she rested her head against his chest. His breaths were shallow but strong. Closing her eyes, she let the sound of it fill her mind. Her body relaxed against his, and she smiled.

Truman opened his eyes and looked around the room. The bathroom door lay in pieces, and an awful smell hung in the air.

A weak chuckle escaped him as he wrapped one arm around Andrea's shoulder. "Damn."

"What?" Andrea asked, looking up at him, her eyes full of alarm. "What's wrong?"

"I don't think I'm going to get my deposit back on the room."

John Ryland lives and writes in Northport, Alabama, with his wife and two sons. His previous works include the novels *Souls Harbor* and *Shatter*, the collection of short stories entitled *Southern Gothic*, and a poetry chapbook, *The Stranger, Poems from the Chair*. You can find his other works in publications such *as Bewildering Stories, The Eldritch Journal, The Writer's Magazine, Otherwise Engaged, The Birmingham Arts Journal, Subterranean Blue*, and others, as well as the online journal *The Chamber Magazine*. His novel *The Man with No Eyes* was released in March 2022.

When not writing or attending various sporting events for his sons, he enjoys gardening, people-watching, and wondering what makes people do the things they do.